Selina Astarre is a graduate of more than one university and has worked in research, TEFL, and the UK education system. While travelling, she met many different friends, teachers and other travellers who encouraged her on her life journey. This book, the first in a series is about the inner journey, a rite of passage and the process of maturation as the soul cries out for proof of the unseen.

For Max with thanks for the encouragement given, and all my friends.

Selina Astarre

BIRRICK'S QUEST FOR THE OTHER WORLD

AUSTIN MACAULEY PUBLISHERS™

LONDON • CAMBRIDGE • NEW YORK • SHARJAH

A CIP catalogue record for this title is available from the British Library.

ISBN 9781398429246 (Paperback)
ISBN 9781398429253 (ePub e-book)

www.austinmacauley.com

First Published 2022
Austin Macauley Publishers Ltd®
1 Canada Square
Canary Wharf
London
E14 5AA

Thanks to Austin Macauley Publishers.

Chapter One

North of the Wall; they lived in the mountains where the days and years passed by, on the quiet side of town, in a hamlet, Malloway. People peacefully tended their gardens. The children studied earnestly and played at the local school. The wind chilled the climate. Often a man might stand in the village square, reading aloud from the bible or some other serious book. This, the Present Lands, in what might be called our time.

Although a winter sun shone, in the evening, the wind whipped around Birrick's ears, his nose was cold, even slightly red. Sitting next to a gnome, beside the pond, Birrick looked menacingly at the goldfish, which he was guarding. There was a spot of rain, and then another. Should he hide in the garden shed where he slept? *"Typical."* thought Birrick. *"Typical of this human world where it rains. Here, on the wrong side of the rainbow. Now, what does she want?"* Birrick asked himself, as the landowner, Sally, turned from her gardening to sit beside Birrick on the wall.

"Humbug," said Birrick, out loud. "Humbug to the rain, humbug to the goldfish and…"

"Yes Birrick?" asked Sally, raising her ginger eyebrows. "Are you humbugging again? You elves are too concerned with your elf problems, and the Other World. So, I have a proposition for you."

Birrick's pointed ears suddenly waggled with delight. "A proposition? A way to get out of here?"

Birrick looked at Sally with interest.

"I have a task for you," Sally rubbed her hands as she spoke.

"What do you want? A lump of gold from the other side of the rainbow?"

"No, nothing as simple as that Birrick. I want you to prove something to me. Then I will let you go free from the curse of the Malloway House, the world of my garden where you guard the goldfish, and from the ties of the Present Lands."

"What do you expect of me?" asked Birrick, shivering in the cold as he eyed the goldfish; two golden, two white, and one black. "What can I do for you?" As Birrick sat shivering, a toad in the pond surfaced for air.

"Bring me the seer's Stone of Second Sight, so that I can see the Other World, and feel satisfied. Then I will believe you and have the proof, Birrick, that I need. When you have done this for me, you will have your heart's desire. You will be a free elf again."

Birrick shook his head in disbelief. "But the Stone of Second Sight, it's difficult to get."

"There will be a way, Birrick," said Sally, looking at him calmly. "Between the now and tomorrow, there is a way for you."

"And if I do this for you, do you swear on your honour, on your goldfish and all you hold dear, that you will let me go? Will you let me go back to the Other World?"

"Yes Birrick, I promise you. You have my word, and my word is as good as my key. I always keep my word and my key, Birrick." Sally sighed; a ray of sunlight suddenly fell on her hair, making it shine a gingery gold. She looked down at Birrick, an elf, not much bigger than a large child. Waiting for Birrick's reply, she sighed again, throwing a stone at a beetle crawling up her ornamental gnome. The stone missed its spot and bounced off into the pond. Birrick inwardly gulped at the thought of his approaching adventure. Glancing at the gnome, it seemed to wink at him, even smile a little. A bird, a nightingale, perched on the fence, turned its attention to Birrick and hopped down to peck at the beetle on the gnome.

"Well, Birrick?" said Sally, impatiently. "What do you say 'to my request?"

"Err, well, of course," said Birrick. "It shall be done."

"Good, then go, get on with it," said Sally, "and remember that the forces of this world and the forces of nature are with you in this quest. It is for a reason."

The nightingale suddenly burst into song, and started to grow, until it was larger than life. She was big enough to carry a passenger. Birrick stood up and mounted the bird.

"Seers have many stones," said Birrick before he and Sally parted company. "The way is through the Cave of Hidden Needles, high up in the Annine's mountains." Stroking the nightingale's head, the bird took off, circling the garden once, so that Birrick could have a final look at Malloway. Sally waved to them, before going inside to look at her runes. There, on her mantelpiece, in the sitting room, was a crystal ball. Sally knew, however, that she could not use the ball without the Stone of Second Sight. She needed it to develop into a decent psychic.

Birrick had a fear of heights. As the nightingale flew higher, the landscape turned from green woodland to rocky grey scree, steep-sloped falls, and snow-topped mountains. Flying over a jagged peek, there was a beautiful waterfall, where a force of water thundered into a deep tarn. Whispering to the bird, the two flew down into the spray of the water, passing through the tumbling wet curtain into a large dark cavern. Landing on the rocky cavern floor, Birrick patted the bird on its head. She gave him a nod, then flew off, leaving Birrick alone in the darkness.

The smell of sulphur reached Birrick's nostrils, and he started to cough. A curl of hot grey smoke followed by several smoke rings drifted towards Birrick. The smoke seemed to have a strange silver sparkle, shining with a luminous light of its own. One of the rings hit Birrick and enveloped him. Birrick felt his temperature rise. A small scaley head, attached to a long body and scaley legs appeared in the dark, crawling on all fours towards the elf. Then another larger scaley dragon approached, just behind the first. Sitting side by side, the two dragons stared at Birrick. The larger dragon opened its mouth, showing several gleaming fangs. The awful creature laughed, letting out a terrible sound, so frightening that Birrick wanted to run. The dragon's collar flared out, as it let out another smoke ring, and a shot of flames hit the floor, burning orange, gold, and red. The second shot of flames made a snake's trail on the floor. A snake of burning flame, which twisted, and grew. As the flames came closer to Birrick, he could not move because he was choking on the fumes, feeling weaker. The dragons whacked their tails; the smaller dragon breathing smoke, the larger beast breathing fire.

As the flames came close to Birrick's face, he sensed the intense heat. The larger dragon laughed again.

"Look," whispered a small voice in Birrick's ear. "Look ahead." Birrick squinted through the hot orange fumes to see him. Behind the dragon stood a man with long dark hair, wearing a red cloak and carrying a long wooden staff that had an animal-shaped head. Several earrings decorated his ears, a collar of white animal bone around his neck. He banged the cave floor with his staff and the dragons parted to let the man through. He seemed to grow taller as he approached Birrick. Putting his staff to the flames, they died back. Birrick's eyebrows were singed with the heat.

"Who are you?" asked Birrick. "Why can't I pass through here?"

"I am the dragon keeper," said the man. "You are a stranger here; strangers need a good enough reason to get into the passage. So, what is your reason, elf? It better be good."

"Otherwise?" asked Birrick.

"Otherwise, no good will come to you, and the dragons will have you," replied the dragon keeper.

"So why?" The man thudded the floor with his staff, impatiently. "Hurry elf! We do not have all of the time left to us."

Birrick inwardly squirmed and said, "I am here to get to the seer."

"Why do you need the seer?" asked the dragon keeper.

"I need his help, to er, to release the message of the Other World. To find a way to get the stone of second sight. It's er, it's important."

The man stamped the floor with his staff and turned away.

13

"Wait, wait," screamed Birrick. "Wait! Come back. I will tell you my secrets, my purpose, I don't want to burn, come back."

Still, the man did not look back. Birrick started to cry. He cried and cried, feeling lonely, lost, and alone. Raising a hand to his face, Birrick looked up. The dragons had gone, with the keeper. The flames died away. A light was shining in the distance. He took courage. A voice whispered in his ear, "Beware, it's time to go." Birrick fled through the cave, into the passage, which had a light in the gloom. He felt that he would know the way. A silver eye winked at him in the dark just as he heard a whistling sound while passing through.

Chapter Two

Suddenly, the voice whispered in Birrick's ear, "Duck." Once again, there was a whistling sound, and a large silver needle flew past his ear, nearly missing him. "Duck again," said the voice. This time, Birrick tried to dodge to the side of the passage. Another needle lodged itself in his hat, and another lodged itself in his shoe. He bent to pick the needle out; it had a human-like eye, which stared at him. Dropping it in fright, Birrick heard the voice again, "Follow me."

"Who are you?" asked Birrick.

"I'm Mr Unreal. The one who is always with you. Can you see the footprints on the floor ahead? You are not the first to try this path; follow the footprints…"

Birrick peered at the floor ahead. Several silvery luminous footprints led a trail down the passage. Just then, a beautiful voice started to sing in a foreign language.

"Follow the prints," repeated Mr Unreal. "Put your feet on the silver path."

Cautiously, Birrick walked along the footprinted path. The needles flew past him; their human eyes glinting and twinkling. The voice of the singer grew louder. Once again, he felt alone and was drawn to the singer's voice which rang out clearly like a bell.

At the end of the passage was a samphire green curtain. An unearthly light came from behind it.

"Draw the curtain," said the singer. "Draw the curtain. I will speak to you."

Thinking that the seer might not be too far off, Birrick lifted his arm and pulled at the seaweed-green curtain. As he did this, several bats flew around him and the singing stopped. Behind the curtain was a young woman, wearing a white dress that was embroidered with gold. Her hair, a fall of golden curls, reached her shoulders. She was sitting at a wooden harp. She seemed to have no eyes but had a lovely face.

"How can you know me?" asked Birrick.

"I see you with my inner eye," replied the young woman, opening a green eye in the middle of her forehead, then shutting it again. "You are Birrick, the elf, you are going on a strange journey. You will need guidance. Ask me anything, anything you like."

"How can I find the seer? Will you guide me?" asked Birrick.

"And why do you seek the seer?"

"To find a way to get the Stone of Second Sight, and by doing this, I will be released from the curse of Malloway."

"The seer lives in the well," said the woman. "I am the Guardian. I guard the way to the seer, and places of spirituality. The seer exacts payment of sorts. He will give you a quest before parting with any stone."

"Where is the well?" asked Birrick.

"Aaah, the Well of Melancholy! It's not far. I don't know what the seer will ask of you, but I can lead you to him."

"Go with her" whispered Mr Unreal. "She will help you."

"Take me. Take me there," pleaded Birrick. "I will do what the seer asks."

"Why so eager?" asked the Guardian.

"To return to the Other World, I must please my keeper; and so, I must find the seer."

"Take my hand," said the Guardian. Birrick looked at her in amazement. She had put on a pair of golden slippers, and begun to disappear feet upwards. "Take my hand, Birrick," she said again, holding out a pale hand with many rings. Holding out his paw, Birrick felt a strange sensation; softness, kindness, and then a feeling of falling. He could no longer see the Guardian but could sense her; her dress, her hand, her presence. Even though they were falling, he felt safe. After some time, he wondered whether they would ever stop. Occasionally a bat fluttered past, or a flying needle winked at them. Holding on to the soft golden Guardian, he felt her arms around him, as they fell through space and time.

Coming to a halt, Birrick realized that he was sitting on something damp, cold, made of stone.

At first, all Birrick could see was a faint golden glow. Slowly, as the Guardian materialized and solidified, he could hear the sound of an owl calling, see the stars in the sky, and a crescent moon above them.

"Aren't you going to take me to the seer?" Birrick asked.

"He lives here," replied the Guardian.

"Eh, here?"

"Yes, look at the wall of the well. We are sitting on it."

Birrick peered downwards. He could see bottomless darkness with a ladder of rusting metal descending into the depths.

"Down there?" asked Birrick.

"Yes."

"Do I have to go all the way down?" Birrick sat there feeling like a drongo. He didn't like heights or depths. Already feeling a strange kind of vertigo, Birrick quivered.

"You only have to go down thirty steps in the ladder. On the thirtieth step is a key in the wall. Take the key and unlock the door there. Go through, and the key will lead you to the seer. Be mindful of the Dracul."

"Dracul?"

"Yes, he preys on youth. And be mindful of Ciarra, the dark one. They will try to take your purpose from you, and to do this, they will try to take the key. The key is magnetic, trust in its power. I must go now, the harp needs my attention. He is calling me. Let go," said the Guardian. "Let go of me."

Birrick released his hold of the soft hand and the Guardian vanished. He heard her singing faintly in the night air, and then silence, nothing.

Birrick picked up a stone and dropped it down the well. He couldn't hear it plop, and he wondered whether the well had a bottom to it. Then an echoing voice emanated from the well.

"Come down, come down," said the echo.

Birrick edged his way around and started clambering down the ladder.

"Watch out," said the voice of Mr Unreal. "Watch out for the slime."

The walls of the well were covered in some type of moss. But just as Birrick descended further, the moss gave way to a seaweed-slime; dripping, moist, unpleasant to touch. Feeling with his foot for a rung in the wall, he slipped on the slime weed, cursing as he held on with his hands alone.

Dangling in the well, Birrick struggled with his feet and the slime. Feeling a solid rung in the wall, he manoeuvred himself further downwards; hand over hand, foot over foot. At the thirtieth rung, a shiny object in the wall caught his attention. It was a strangely ornate key, glowing with a light of its own. Reaching out carefully, the key seemed to jump into Birrick's hand. He heard tinkling laughter and a rope of slime slapped him in the face. Birrick could taste the salt of the weed.

A door opened in the wall of the well, and Birrick edged his way towards the open entrance. With one foot on the ladder and the other in the doorway, Birrick grabbed ahold of the dangling rope, pulling himself through the opening. Again, he heard the laugh, a child's laugh.

Mr Unreal spoke in his ear, "Be afraid. There is a lot of power in this place."

Birrick ran as fast as he could to get away from the laughter and the slime.

He heard the echo again, "Come on down." It was a man's voice.

In the dank, slimy passage, Birrick ran on into the darkness. Tussling with slime weed slapping at him, his feet sliding on the weedy surface, Birrick smacked his face on a solid surface and fell onto the floor. The laughter sounded, and Birrick found himself looking into the eyes of a dark-haired child, dressed in black.

"Hello, Birrick," said the child. "Pleased to meet you. Give me your key and I will guide you. You are looking for the seer, aren't you? I'm Ciarra. Say my name, Birrick, say my name, and call me your friend. I know you, Birrick. I know what you want, and I want the same."

Birrick looked at Ciarra, and suddenly he heard Mr Unreal's voice, "Do not give in to her. She will do you harm."

"Go away, Ciarra," said Birrick. "The key is my guide."

"I am your friend," insisted Ciarra, smiling and showing bad teeth. Birrick looked at the key, it glowed red. Raising his hand, he tapped Ciarra lightly on the head with the luminous key. She let out a high-pitched cry. Turning into a snail before Birrick's eyes, Ciarra slimed off down the passage.

"Birrick!" boomed out the echoing man's voice. "Birrick! get up, turn and see!"

Birrick pulled himself up onto his feet and turned. There was a mirror, where before there had been slime and rock. The large full-length mirror reflected, not Birrick, but a man with grey hair, in a purple robe. The man beckoned to Birrick. "Join me," said the man.

"How?" asked Birrick.

"Step forward four paces and point the key at your heart. Say the magical words, 'sacerdotes video volo parlo'. You will be allowed to enter."

"But there's a mirror in the way," said Birrick.

"No, you will enter." A hand extended from the mirror, beckoning Birrick, and ushering him to pass.

With that, a whisp, a small white ghostly face appeared in the passage.

"I am the whisp of the seer. He will let you through," murmured the whisp.

"Strange way to walk through a wall," said Birrick out loud.

"Try," said the whisp.

So, pointing the key at his chest, and muttering the magical words, Birrick took four steps forward, stepping through the mirror, and into the seer's cell.

The seer looked old, his eyes a brilliant blue, his face pale, wrinkled with wisdom. On his feet were pointed velvety shoes, and in his hair were plaits and beads. He wore a long red and gold silk scarf, draped around his shoulders.

"You are looking for something?" asked the seer. "I am a giver to those who are good enough. What is your request?"

"I am looking for the Stone of Second Sight. My keeper wants the stone. She wants to see the Other World before letting me go free. Can you help me please?"

The seer smiled at Birrick and he felt a glimmer of hope.

"Let me see. The Stone of Second Sight, which I could give you a quest for, can only be given to those who are pure in heart, which means that you must pass my test, to prove that you are good enough."

"But…" said Birrick, "But the key has already brought me here, so surely I am enough?"

"No, no. There must be a test."

"Well, what is it, this test? Tell me what I must do."

"If I set you this test, you must complete it. Otherwise, you will be doomed. Doomed to a life without magic, without the Other World, and doomed to be a servant forever."

Birrick swallowed, and then spoke, "Alright, so tell me."

"You must go to the hidden garden and bring back a rose that is truly white."

"Why white?"

"Because, if your heart is good enough, then the rose will turn white, pure white. If, however, the rose is dark in some way, this indicates a dark heart, an impure soul, and I will know."

"Could it be a plastic rose?" Birrick naively asked.

"No, nor silk. It must be a living rose, just as you are a living being. Should the rose be impure, you will be refused, Birrick."

Birrick looked sadly at the seer, feeling a lump in his throat. He thought of the Other World, of crumpets with honey, and his mother, an old elf playing tunes on cobwebs.

"What do you say, Birrick?"

"Yes then, I take you on your word," said Birrick. "I will return."

"Go through the mirror. It is the only way, and keep the key with you. It will be enough to ensure your safety."

"Won't I need to put the key back in the well?"

"No, another key has already taken its place."

Birrick looked over his shoulder at the mirror.

"Don't look back. Look forward Birrick," said the seer.

The mirror gleamed brightly, showing Birrick his reflection. The seer didn't appear in the mirror. Pointing the key, Birrick stepped through the mirror into the dark slimy tunnel. Turning around to look, the mirror was no longer there.

"Run Birrick, run," whispered the voice of Mr Unreal. "Dracul the vampire is watching you. Even the rats see you here, even the snails know you. They can only see you while you are in the dark, so run, run."

A tall dark figure, a man in black jeans and a sweater with dark hair stepped out of the shadows. "Birrick," said the man. "Birrick." His voice was quiet and low, with a threat in it. "Birrick, you have great talent. You are promising." The man smiled, showing his fangs. "Would you like an easier way to get what you want? Would you like an easy ride in life? I would like to help you."

Birrick looked up at the man, he had a pale face, with dark rings around his eyes. The man reached out a hand to stroke Birrick's cheek.

"Dracul," whispered Mr Unreal, "Dracul." Birrick felt a sting in his face as the man stroked him.

"Dracul wants your heart, Birrick, Dracul wants the key," whispered Mr Unreal. "Hide it, you have power. Run Birrick, run."

Birrick shivered as a cold wind swept through the tunnel. Walking quickly, then breaking into a run, Birrick moved as fast as his elfin legs would carry him. Leaping, scrambling, running for all he was worth, the entrance opened up before him, and Birrick made a final surge. Slipping on a piece of slimy weed, he fell over the edge of the doorway, flailing as he fell downwards. Grasping at ropes of slime which slipped through his fingers, Birrick hurtled wet and screaming down through the well. Where would he land? Would he be good enough to pass the seer's test?

Chapter Three

Bump! Birrick came into contact with the bottom, or what he thought was the bottom. Jolting to a stop, he opened his eyes. Finding himself on a grassy hump, he lay there for a while. First, he tried to move his right leg, then his left. Gingerly raising himself onto his legs, he assessed that he had no broken bones, but had strands of slime on his clothes.

"Hello," said a voice. Swivelling around to look, there was a small man, a kind of a leprechaun, jumping on and off a coin-making machine.

"Lucky you landed on my grassy cushion, and not in my soup," said the leprechaun, jumping on his machine to press out coins. "Or even worse, you could have landed in that cow pat. Someone must be watching over you."

"I am protected," said Birrick, looking curiously at the small man in the bright sunshine.

"Protected, huh?"

"Yes, is this the Hidden Garden? It's beautiful enough." Birrick looked around him, at the many flowers, herbs, bushes. A cow stood nearby, munching on the grass, and a rainbow seemed to grow behind it.

"Well, what's it to you?"

"Do you have any roses, white roses?" asked Birrick eagerly.

"No, I specialize in gold coins, because, of course, I'm a leprechaun. My name's Oleg."

"Is this the end of the rainbow? How can I find a pure white rose bush?" Birrick enquired anxiously.

"Ask the hobgoblin who lives on Hobgoblin Hill. He cultivates a few roses, or even try the Queen of the Bees. They'll know about horticulture, bees, don't they? Would you like some mushroom soup?"

"Soup? With croutons?" Birrick thought of creamy mushroom soup, French style.

"No, with weeds, I don't grow croutons."

"Alright, I'll try some," said Birrick.

Oleg dismounted from the coin machine and took two bowls out of thin air, dishing soup into them from the large cauldron which bubbled away beside the coin contraption. The Leprechaun handed Birrick a bowl, sipping from his own.

Birrick looked at his soup, it seemed green with weeds or herbs floating in it. He sniffed then swallowed a mouthful. Spluttering at the sour-tasting weeds, Birrick put the bowl down.

"Where can I find the hobgoblin?" Birrick asked. "Could you give me some gold to bribe him with?" Birrick looked at the coins, trying to work out their value.

"Certainly not" barked the Leprechaun. "You have to try harder than that!"

"Then how can I get the rose?"

"You can try. You are not guaranteed success in everything," remarked the little old man. "Walk on from here, turn left into the forest of pointed mushrooms, pass under the white tree, and finally walk or crawl up the hill with a flag at its peak. There is a house, on the hill; knock on the door; four times or maybe five times. The hobgoblin might answer, and may even have some roses for you if you are polite."

"And the Queen Bee, where is she? You don't normally see bees at this time of the year."

"She's in her hive, at the foot of the hill. Now off you go on your way. I have enough to do with turning day into night, making coins, and mushroom soup! If you don't want that soup, I'm having it. Goodbye!"

Snatching up the bowl, Oleg downed the soup in one gulp, before jumping back onto his machine to continue pressing out peculiar gold coins. One of the coins rolled in Birrick's direction. He picked it up, looking at the strange design; a set of runic characters on the front, an imprint of Oleg on the back. Putting the coin in his pocket, Birrick turned in the direction of what seemed like a forest. As he got closer, he could see a man bending down to pick some sort of plant. The man, who seemed young, had a bearded face and a large nose. He had a large sack on his back and was dressed in corduroys. Birrick walked on, drawing nearer. Getting closer, Birrick could see that the man was picking pointed mushrooms or toadstools, smelling them, then putting them in his sack. The mushrooms made a squealing noise as they were picked, indicating that they were flavoursome. Some of the mushrooms seemed as tall as Birrick.

The bearded man came up to Birrick and asked, "What are you going to pay me? You must pay to pass here."

"But I haven't any money," said Birrick, trying to sound innocent.

"Yes you have," said the man looking at Birrick squarely; one hand on his hips, the other on his sack. "You have elf, you've been talking to that leprechaun. Anyways, elves have elfin gold, we all know that. Give me a coin and I will let you pass. Or go on and perform an elvish spell for me, magic me some elvish gold." The man smiled, greedily.

"I could give you a four-leaf clover coin!" Birrick replied, feeling in his pockets for the smallest of his coins. "It's very lucky." Birrick fished out the coin, holding out a rose gold coin in the shape of a clover.

Biting it to see if the coin was genuine, the bearded man pointed into the forest. "You might find what you want through there. Some do. Whatever, don't pick the toadstools. That's my business, see." The man shook his fist, walking off to pick some more.

Soon enough, as Birrick walked through the trees and toadstools, he came across a sign, 'Hobgoblin Hill, this way'. The sign pointed Birrick in the direction of a narrow trail, blazed with carved stakes at different points. Birrick took a toffee out of his pocket, unwrapped it, and dropped the paper on the wood floor.

"This is the way, your way," whispered Mr Unreal in Birrick's ear. Passing by various old, gnarled trees, some with faces carved into the bark, a gathering light began to filter through the trees. A tree painted marble white became visible in a clearing. "Hide," said Mr Unreal. A large bird swooped through the trees, trying to claw Birrick as it flew past him. "Once you get to the white tree, you will be safe," said Mr Unreal. Birrick tried to hurry on but found himself sinking into the soft earth, so soft that it seemed like a quagmire of sticky mud. Each time Birrick tried to lift a foot, it became harder. Struggling on, and the more he struggled, the more he sank. Birrick soon found himself up to the waist in mud. He tried to grab at an overhead branch, but his arms weren't long enough. Sinking quickly, Birrick knew that he had to get to the white tree, but he could barely move in the mud which was sucking him in.

The large bird flew past again, cawing loudly, and came to rest beside the quagmire. It looked keenly at Birrick with its head on one side. A woman's face appeared in the mud.

"Your crimes are sucking you in," said the face. "They will devour you in time, as will the birds, the earthworms, and the creatures of the forest. Or recant; swear to do good, do us some good, and we will let you leave."

"How can I recant?" wailed Birrick. "I'm stuck in the mud!"

"After me, I swear to be green, and keep the woods clean."

"I swear," whinged Birrick. "I swear."

"Louder," said the woman.

"Alright then. I swear, I swear, I swear," shouted Birrick.

"I find you meaningful," said the woman. "Even believable."

An overhanging tree branch lowered itself within Birrick's reach. He grabbed it and levered himself out of the mud, which dried on him, leaving his clothes covered in brown dust.

Birrick brushed the dust off his clothes. The mud patch dried up into a brown earthy surface. "I want to be clean; I want to be green," said Birrick out loud. Shaking the dust off his feet, he walked into the white tree, bumping his head on its trunk, and paused under its barren white branches.

A large-looking bumble bee flew past Birrick, with a light in its bottom that glowed a jelly orange. Another bee hovered nearby and settled on Birrick's shoulder, and several more came to hover around him. The air was thickening with bees and a swarm was gathering around the tree. The swarm began to move on, taking Birrick with it. He was afraid that he would be stung, so put his hands in his pockets. The whole moving, breathing, humming mass came to a stop at a large beehive, on which a very large female bee was sitting. While the drones filtered into the hive to make honey, the Queen Bee raised herself to look Birrick in the face.

"Yezzzzz?" buzzed the female bee. "Yezzz elf-man, what is your purpose here? Have you come to help us, the bees, or to destroy our peace?"

"Er...er...where...where can I find the hobgoblin who keeps roses, please?" Birrick looked at the bee and the bee looked at Birrick. He knew that all sorts of cures came from bee-stings. However, he also knew that he didn't want to try a sting to find out.

"Roses are expensive," said the bee. "Take this honeycomb in return for what you seek. The hill is that way, along the gravel path. Would you like to try a sting juice cocktail?" The bee gave Birrick a serious glare as she handed him the honeycomb. "Or perhaps, some honey mead? I could invite you for a parlour tea."

"No, no. Thanks," said Birrick, taking the sweet treat. Turning to go, he knocked the hive, dislodging hundreds of drones that gathered in a cloud. The bees sang angrily. Birrick started to run up the gravel track, panting and cursing. Hundreds of bees followed him, too closely for comfort. As fast as Birrick ran, the bees seemed to catch up with him.

Suddenly there was a large crack of thunder, followed by a flash of sheet lightning. Quick as quicksand, the bees disappeared just as the rain fell, drenching Birrick through to his underwear.

The rain fell so heavily that Birrick couldn't run. He trudged slowly; the raindrops rivuletting around his ears and down his neck. Climbing the white gravel path which led up an incline, another flash of lightning struck. Birrick looked up; luminous in the storm was a woman with golden hair, wearing a white robe and gold sandals.

"Here, Birrick," said the vision. "I am Acha. Take this." She held out an apple. "I give you this gift, use it wisely. You will benefit if you act with wisdom. You are old for your years." There was another flash, and the golden woman was gone. Birrick felt in his pocket. He could touch the key, and another object, a round smooth thing. Taking it out in his hand, he held a half-red half-green apple. Taking a bite, the apple quickly turned into a pure red, delicious apple. Chomping through to the core, Birrick noticed a pattern of a rose etching in the seeds. Taking the seeds out, he threw the empty core away over his shoulder and deposited the seeds in his pocket. A cold north wind was blowing down the hillside. A few yards away, Birrick could see a rickety tin shed, with a grey curtain at the window. Walking up to the shed, Birrick tried to open the door, thinking that he would shelter inside.

Chapter Four

Opening the shed door, inside was a stove, burning brightly. A hedgehog, a largeish creature, sat on a wooden chair. The shed had boxes stacked against the walls. In one corner was a mattress for a bed. The shed was warm. Birrick opened his mouth to question. The hedgehog beat him to it.

"And who is this in my shed? Don't say, the storm has brought you here. Washed out, huh? And in need of a rest? Travellers are welcome, come in. I will give you a potion with a portion of my mind. Come in, come in. Stop letting in the wind and wasting time."

Birrick stepped inside, glad to be somewhere that seemed safe and warm.

"Is the hobgoblin's house nearby?" he asked.

"The hobgoblin? If you're looking for the hobgoblin, then you're after something people always are. What are you after, friend?"

"Er… The rose. The rose for the pure-hearted, and the secret way to get back to the Other World."

"Hah, you'll be lucky!" said the hedgehog. "I suppose you think that pigs can fly as well."

"Well."

"Well, they can. Let me see, I think I have just the potion for you. Look in that top box over there. Bring it down for me, the one marked 'Extras'."

Birrick swivelled around to look at the boxes. They seemed dilapidated, covered in dust, finger-marks, and labels. Inspecting the pile, one box which looked particularly dog-eared had a strangely scripted label, Birrick squinted and scrunched his eyes up trying to read it. Through the blur, he could make out the words, 'Extra Special'. Thinking that might be it, he tugged at the box, lifting it carefully. Lifting the flap lid, there were several bottles inside.

"Over here, bring it here," said the hedgehog.

Gingerly taking the box over to the stove where the hedgehog sat, Birrick placed it on the floor.

"Now let me see. That one's a poison," said the hedgehog, lifting out a rectangular-shaped blue bottle. "This one's a lung tonic. This, what's this? Dear me, vanilla essence. Now here, here. I think this is what we need." The hedgehog held up a transparent pale green bottle with a strange particularly wavy pattern on it. The hedgehog uncorked it and sniffed.

"There we are," said the hedgehog, coughing. "This is what you want. Drink this." The hedgehog handed the pale bottle over to Birrick. He looked at it dumbfounded.

"Drink it?"

"Yes."

The pale liquid inside had a lemony smell. Birrick took a sip.

"All of it, young elf. All of it. You're too big a creature for just a sip."

Swigging the liquid down in two gulps, Birrick coughed, then it started. Birrick had a tingling sensation in his feet.

Looking down, yellow feathers were sprouting from his ankles. Then his arms tingled. Looking at his wrists, he saw that fluffy feathers were protruding there.

"Help," said Birrick. "I don't want to be a bird."

"Oh, it's only temporary. This way you will fly away from trouble. You will get what you want this time," said the hedgehog, and laughed. "Anyway, yellow feathers are quite becoming with that green jacket of yours. Now, wait a few more seconds until the transformation is complete. You will be able to fly above the storm and get to the hobgoblin's house easily. Just in time for tea! Now can you say anything better than that?"

The hedgehog was smiling quite brightly, his brown eyes gleaming in the light from the stove.

"You're ready now, open the door and fly away. I need to rest. Be gone elf, hop onto the next wind. Go on, be gone."

The door to the shed banged open, and as a gust of wind came to him, it took Birrick with it. Stumbling, then flapping his feathers and flying, he soared as he gained his balance; his poise in the air. Flying higher, the wind took his breath away and the storm and the hut were left behind. He passed a gaggle of flying geese, a murder of crows. As he swooped forwards, over the green fell below, he spied a cottage with a garden and a fountain. There was a flag hoisted on the roof, skull, and crossbones.

"That's it," Birrick muttered to himself. Making a steep descent onto the back lawn, Birrick posed for a few seconds, to admire himself in the garden pond. The feathers fell onto the gravel pathway as Birrick made his way to the compost heap where a wizened old man, wearing a naval outfit, was dumping his household leftovers into his compost bin.

33

"Ahem," said Birrick, clearing his throat. "Ahem."

"Yes, ahem?" The grumpy voice of the old man, a hobgoblin, indicated that he was not too pleased. He took out his pipe, wiped it on his navy jacket sleeve, then sucked on it. "Well, ahem?"

"Er... Birrick. The name's Birrick," said Birrick nervously. "I'm, er... here on a quest."

"Best come on inside, and I'll see if I can help you with what you want." The hobgoblin looked at Birrick and nodded. "This way."

Strutting on ahead, the wizened man marched on into his cottage, which had spider webs at the windows, and a furry long-haired Persian black cat waiting at the door. Once inside, the man sat on a rocking chair, with the cat on his lap. At one half of the main room was a curtain, cutting the room in two.

"Sit down," said the hobgoblin. "Have you come to steal my fish?"

"No, I don't eat fish," said Birrick.

"But you don't need to eat them to steal them. I have my favourite shubunkins in the fountain. Some people would steal those."

Birrick blushed, feeling uncomfortable at the thought of the garden at Malloway, the pond, the fishes.

"You have come here for something; I know that elf. Everyone who comes here comes for something. You have mentioned a quest, you are a seeker of fortune or fate. So then." The man stroked the cat and played with its ears. "So?"

"Roses, white roses, do you have any? The pure sort. If I give you this piece of honeycomb, can I have a pure white rose in return?"

"Honeycomb, huh? Give it here." Birrick handed the honeycomb over. The hobgoblin took it and fed it to his cat.

"The everlasting rose, hey. You want the everlasting rose; I can't give those away easily." The cat devoured the honeycomb, licking its paws. "You haven't told me everything. You are from the Other World elf, why aren't you in the Other World now?"

The hobgoblin rocked backward and forwards quite violently on the chair so that his cat jumped off his knee.

Birrick looked at his boots and swallowed.

"I was thrown out, banned to be made to do good. I was caught smoking, and I blew out the candles on someone else's birthday cake. I sang out of tune, and out of time. I smashed my violin up in a fit of bad temper. Gabriel, Raphael, and Uriel sent me away in disgrace."

"Couldn't you appeal to the Archangel Michael?"

"He turned me away, said I had to reform."

"You must have done worse than that. I don't believe you."

"I cursed my father."

"Why?"

"I never knew him; he ran away before I can remember."

"You knew your mother?"

"Yes, she's still there, playing tunes on cobwebs and singing in the choir."

"Do you miss her?"

"Yes, yes. She was old and kind. She's my mother."

"Well then, I will ask something of you, before I make up my mind about you, elf. By the way, what's your name?"

"Birrick."

"Well, Birrick." The hobgoblin got up, pacing back and forth. "I used to have a wife and child. When I sailed the seas, I'd look forward to coming home to be with them again. But, in these parts, there's a problem."

"Oh?"

"Yes; border reivers, stealing, killing, kidnapping. While I was away, the reivers came and stole my wife and child. We are north of the Wall here."

"The Wall?"

"Yes, and they took my family away, over the Wall, stole my gold, and ransacked my home. They asked for a ransom which I could not pay. Do you think you could bring me a new wife and child? There's a village in the woods. Go there, steal me, or snatch me a wife, a child, blonde-haired with blue eyes. Take them with your elfin powers, bring them to me. That way I might trust you Birrick. You might get the rose that way, and then I might feel safe."

"I see," said Birrick. "And what if I fail?"

"Well," said the hobgoblin and shrugged. "Are you going?"

Birrick was surprised at the request. He screwed up his pointed face and wiggled his pointed ears. Looking at the hobgoblin, he asked, "Where can I find them for you?"

"Aaah now. Walk north, follow the north star, you will come to a clearing in the woods. There's a small village. The women are very pretty there. Bring me what I ask, go Birrick. She must be fair in form and face, full of charm and grace. Now go!"

The hobgoblin took Birrick by the arm, pushed him out the door, and slammed it in his face with such force that the fish-shaped metal door knocker rattled. Looking at the door,

Birrick noticed a spy hole. Putting his face to the hole, he tried to peer through, blinking right back at him was the hobgoblin. The door shook as the goblin banged on it from inside. Stunned, Birrick looked at the sky. He could see the north star above the plough constellation. "Can I fly?" Birrick wondered. He tried to flap his arms, but nothing happened. The feathers had gone. Vanished. Turning into the darkness, Birrick walked on, the north wind whipping his clothes and his face. By the light of the moon, he could see a shadow on the horizon. Getting closer, he knew that he was approaching the woods, and he felt a strange foreboding. A knot of fear; the tension in his stomach as he thought of what he had to do.

Coming into the darkness of the trees, the leaves seemed to whisper to him, "Go away, you are not wanted here. These are the Forbidden Woods." The rustling sound was haunting. A small creature, a bat, flew at Birrick. Then it pounced on a rabbit, which had been hiding among the leaves on the ground. The bat perched on the back of the unfortunate animal, digging its fangs into the neck fur. Birrick paused to watch; the bat seemed to have a white human face and dark eyes. The rabbit did not struggle but grew weak as the bat sucked its lifeblood. Feeling sorry for the rabbit, Birrick picked up a stone to throw at the bat. Before he could aim, the bat sucked his last, jumped off the unconscious rabbit, and flew close to Birrick, hovering as the two stared each other in the face. Changing into a man, with dark hair and dark clothes, the bat metamorphosed into Dracul, standing in front of Birrick and blocking the way.

Taken aback, Birrick found himself shivering as the man looked down on him. "Hello elf, I have been waiting for you. I will take you to the village, I know the way. Take my hand,

I will show you." The Dracul had a low husky voice, and he took Birrick by the arm. He walked very quickly so that Birrick could barely keep up, all sorts of animals, night creatures seemed to dash across their path, badgers, moles, even an owl which flew close, hooting a warning, then flying off. A branch caught Birrick in the face. "Ow", he said, putting his hand to the scratch. There was blood on his face.

"Interesting," said Dracul, stroking the scratch and tasting the blood. The scratch healed immediately.

The sound of folk music reached Birrick's ears on the night air; pipe music, fiddles, laughing, singing.

"We are getting closer," said Dracul, following the sound of celebration, the two stumbled, then stopped. Birrick could make out lights between the trees, then stone cottages.

"It's here?" he asked.

"Yes, here," replied Dracul. Walking on to get a good look, many men were dancing around a bonfire, while women in a green folk outfit sang and clapped in time as the two musicians, men with handkerchiefs on their heads, played the fiddle and the pipes.

Birrick could smell roasting hog, and the rich smell seemed to emanate from the stone cottage in front of him. Quietly going up to the window to look inside, Birrick could see a young woman; blonde, playing with a fair-haired child, as a hog roasted on the open fire within. Watching the two playing, Birrick felt a sadness, should he take them, what then? The two were playing a clapping game and singing. "You have bad blood," whispered Mr Unreal in Birrick's ear. A pang of pain hit him in the neck. Dracul was sucking on Birrick's blood.

Birrick tried to push the Dracul away but was not strong enough. "No, let me help you," whispered Dracul as he sucked. Birrick moaned with fear, and a white pain ran through him. "There now, that's better," said Dracul. "Now how do you feel?" He smiled showing his crooked fangs. Birrick rubbed his neck, looked up at the Dracul, then turned to look at the hearthside scene in the cottage. Suddenly feeling useless, Birrick tapped on the window. The pair inside did not hear him and continued playing.

"Take them," whispered Mr Unreal. "Take them, you know how. It's easier to do evil, it's easier this way."

Looking at the pair playing innocently, Birrick turned away, walking back into the shadows of the night.

"You have seen what you want?" asked Dracul, following him.

"Yes, but elfin magic is meant to do good, not bad." Birrick felt quite upset. "I can't take them, it's wrong. I feel tired."

"Then I will lead you out of the woods. Get on my back, you will be weak for a while."

Birrick climbed onto Dracul's back, his arms around Dracul's shoulders. Speeding on, Dracul carried Birrick to the edge of the woods, where there was a ruined ivy-covered folly.

"This is my home," said Dracul. "Would you like to come inside?"

Birrick slipped down, and the moonlight shone on Dracul's eyes, teeth, and pale skin.

"I won't hurt you," said the Dracul.

Birrick sighed, he thought of the hobgoblin and Sally in Malloway.

"Leave this place," whispered Mr. Unreal in Birrick's ear. "leave, leave."

Obeying the sinister voice, and in a state of near exhaustion, Birrick stumbled then hurried in the direction of the hobgoblin's house on Hobgoblin Hill.

"Stupid Birrick, no good elf, you will never get what you want," Birrick muttered to himself, crying, and cursing. "No good, drongo, noodle, loser, elf magic humbug." As he continued, the wind behind him, Mr Unreal did not whisper another word.

Hobgoblin Hill had a series of steps on the other side, which Birrick tried to mount. Somehow he couldn't get past the tenth step and kept on ending at the bottom again. Two children, a boy, and a girl joined at the hip, were carrying a pail up the hill passed him on the steps.

"Wait, wait," called Birrick after them, "help me, who are you?"

They turned to look at him, they were joined at the hip, sharing three legs.

"We are the children of the night; we carry water for the hobgoblin's fountain."

"Let me carry the pail for you," said Birrick, and taking the pail from them, he made it to the top of the hill. Looking around at the top of the steps, the Siamese twins were gone, vanished into the night.

Chapter Five

Knocking on the door of Hobgoblin Cottage, the inhabitant goblin opened it, to stare at Birrick. Birrick stared back. Feeling suddenly as if his heart was in the bucket of water, Birrick leaned against the doorpost trying to think of an excuse.

"Well?" barked the goblin.

"I er…I er…" Then gulping and garbling the words he blurted out, "I couldn't do it." His heart felt cold. He looked at the floor, the walls, the goblin. A tear started to trickle down his nose, a feeling of shame came over Birrick.

The goblin was quiet, scratching his hairy chin. "Put that water in the fountain, then come inside. I have something for you."

Birrick did as he was told. Entering the cottage with the empty pail, Birrick could see the clock with the many eyes hanging over the mantelpiece. The time was midnight.

The goblin vanished behind an old curtain drawn over half of the room. He made a few grunting noises, then reappeared with his left hand behind his back.

"Sit down," said the goblin. "Here." he extended his left arm, in his left hand was a red and white rose. Birrick reached out to take it. As his fingers touched the stalk, the petals transformed to a completely pure white rose. A sound came from the cuckoo clock beside the door, and the cuckoo flew around the room, landing on the goblin's shoulder. Suddenly, all the clocks chimed twelve, a grandfather clock which stood tall in the corner, the clock with many eyes and the cuckoo clock. The goblin smiled at Birrick.

"There, you have it now. You are good enough."

"Am I?" asked Birrick.

"Yes, never doubt yourself. Stay here the night and go on your journey tomorrow morning. You, Birrick, will not be a noodle. Your life's quest will not be a vain one. However, many things will come to you. There are still challenges ahead."

Birrick looked at the clock with many green eyes, the hands were whirring around, so many times a minute.

"It's a second sight clock," said the goblin. "The small hand passes around once a second, but it still tells the right time. Ask it a question, and it will answer you. Go on, ask, I know you want to."

Birrick got up to get a closer look at the clock, drawing closer he could see a thin, mealy-mouth in the clock face.

"What is my mother doing now?" he asked.

The clock face groaned, then the mealy lips opened, "She is preparing for Christmas, and is kept very busy."

"Does she think of me?"

"Yes, she does."

Birrick smiled a small elfin smile and tucked the white rose into his jacket buttonhole.

The hobgoblin went to the stove and took a tray of oaty jumping jack flapjacks from the oven.

"Take some," he said to Birrick, and two flapjacks somersaulted into Birrick's outstretched hand.

"Stay the night," said the goblin. "You will be tired, you can leave in the morning. Drink this." The hobgoblin handed Birrick a large mug of frothy hot chocolate with cream. He ate and drank, feeling somewhat warmer inside. The goblin put a blanket over Birrick as he sat on the old comfy chair, soon he was asleep.

In his sleep, Birrick began to dream…

First, he was flying again, with wings at his feet and his arms. Flying towards the Wizard's Well, Malloway House, and the Other World. As the Present Lands passed beneath him, and the stars above, he was surrounded by bats, many black bats. The bats flew around him, and then two dragons, with claws, wings, and teeth joined them. A sign appeared in the sky, a circle containing a triangle, in burning gold, and a green eye opened within the triangle, blinking at Birrick as he flew. Suddenly, Birrick was falling, falling towards the darkness of the well, which seemed to be below.

"Ahem, and have you got it?" said a voice in his ear. Birrick struggled with himself, then awoke. In his sleepy state he heard another whispering voice, Mr Unreal, "To enter the Other World through the Eternal Doorway, your aura must be gold. Do you think you are good enough now?" Then the sound of laughter haunted him, so he stood up, shaking his arms and legs, to check that he was in control.

"Well, have you got the rose?" asked the goblin again. "For I certainly won't be giving you another."

Birrick paused, then lifted his jacket off the back of the chair, in the top buttonhole was a whiter than white rose.

"Hmm," said the hobgoblin, "and take this." He held out a silver medal on a chain. "Take it."

Birrick held out his elf-paw and took the piece of jewellery. There was some writing on it, in a strange script.

"What does it say? What does it mean?" Birrick asked the goblin.

"The inscription on one side is in Hobgoblinish. It means 'blessed is the one who believes'. On the other side are the names of the important Archangels, and the important hobgoblins."

"Oh," said Birrick in surprise. "I knew that there were important angels, but who are the important hobgoblins, please? I've never heard of that before."

The hobgoblin smiled, showing crooked teeth. "The important hobgoblins are Finan, Fergal, and Sioune. I am Finan. Although, perhaps you didn't realise. Put it on. The blessing will protect you."

There was a whistling noise as the on-the-hob kettle started to boil. The hobgoblin, Finan, went to make tea, while Birrick put on the jewellery, touching the medal he felt a strange sensation, sending a mild electric shock up his arm. Looking at the second sight clock, the eyes opened, blinked, then closed again. It was 8.30 am.

"I had a dream," said Birrick, "and I fell from the sky, away from the Other World."

"Never stop believing. It is what is in our minds that is important. This is how we create our reality. Your mind will get stronger as you struggle, and then you will cease to struggle with yourself. Sugar?"

Asked the hobgoblin, "Milk?"

"Er, just milk thanks." Finan brought over a tray with mugs of tea and a plate of singing hinny muffins, which hummed a tune until Birrick bit into one, causing the muffin chorus to cease.

Birrick finished off the plate of cakes, then asked, "I need to get to the Well of Melancholy, also known as the Wizard's Well. Is there a quick way, perhaps a secret route that is safe? I have already had a problem or two with bats." Birrick looked at Finan, Finan looked back, clearing his throat.

"There could be another way, through the hermit's cave. Though I haven't gone that way for a long time myself. If you go through the hermit's cave, there is a way to get to the Seer, going down past Darkening Castle, along the riverbank. Turn left as you leave here, walk into the wind along the south side of the hill, and you will see the castle in the distance on a rise. Aim to the right of the castle, walking down to the riverside. Walk the way that the river flows, and you will find the hermit in his cave. If the hermit allows you through the cave, there is an easy route to the Seer. But beware, the hermit has a six-headed dog, which gets hungry from time to time. The dog is called Tolcan. Feed him, and you will pass."

"Does the hermit have a name?" asked Birrick.

"The hermit is the hermit with no name, so don't ask. He forgot that a long time ago. Don't annoy him, just smile." The hobgoblin's eyes gleamed. "It is believing which will carry you through successfully, magic or knowledge is of no use without belief. Look into the flames of the fire, Birrick. What can you see there? Tell me."

Birrick turned his gaze to the fireplace and the glowing flames. An image materialized in the glow, a man with red hair, wearing a golden key. The man was wringing his hands with worry. He picked up a staff with a blade at one end, then disappeared.

"I saw a man. He was unhappy," said Birrick.

"Did he have red hair and a staff?" asked the goblin.

"Yes," Birrick replied.

"That was Lamnnguin, the Blade. He will come to you, or you to him. When the time is right, you will be challenged. Now go, your destiny awaits you. Anyway, it is a fine day, I must get on with the gardening."

So Birrick left Hobgoblin House, journeying on, and walking into the wind, just as the hobgoblin told him to. The mist shimmered on the grass, and Birrick felt hopeful that he would reach the Seer by fate.

Chapter Six

Coming down by the side of Darkening Castle, a majestic walled construction of stone, the wind whispered to Birrick, and he whistled down the wind. Along the riverbank which he strolled along were weeds, grasses, and the odd mallard duck. There was a barking noise, and Birrick froze to the spot. A dog bounded past him with a stick in its mouth. Running after it was an out-of-breath jogger.

"Hello," puffed the jogger. "We don't bite." Birrick relaxed, walking on a little further. Suddenly a howl erupted through the morning air, and a terrible clanking sound, of a chain.

Birrick pushed the grass away. There was a large, black and white dog with six heads, a kind of pit terrier, snarling, drooling, and pulling on its chain. Birrick closed his eyes tightly, trying to make himself believe. The largest of the dog's heads was only inches away from him. Panic and fear began to churn in Birrick's stomach, his hair standing on end from his toes to his eyebrows. "Believe," whispered the wind, "Believe." Opening his eyes, Birrick saw a pomegranate at the side of his path. Picking it up, he threw it at the dog. The fruit met the mark, lodging itself in the dog's throat. Choking and gasping, the dog rolled onto its back in agony. As it writhed, frothing at its six mouths, Birrick tiptoed by. Sitting at a table, beside a hazel tree, in front of a crack in the rocks, was a man with a grey beard, bending over a scroll of paper. There was a quill in the hand of the man, whom Birrick took to be the hermit.

The hermit wore a rough brown wool robe, letting out a heavy sigh, he turned his steely grey eyes on Birrick.

"Yes, what is it elf?" asked the hermit.

"What is your name?" asked Birrick, curious.

"I have no time for names, I have no name," said the hermit. "I can't remember, or at least I don't want to. I've been here a long time. Why do you disturb me?"

"I need to pass, I need to pass quickly, to get to the Seer. I am told you know the way, hermit?"

"Ah, well, and you er, have some special purpose?"

"Yes."

"That's all very well for you, but what's in it for me? Look at my dog, elf, he seems quite unhappy, choking on a pomegranate. You are disturbing the peace! You are disturbing me; I have been decorating this scroll for quite a few hundred years! Why should I let you through to the Seer? He's a busy man, and so am I."

The hermit folded his arms, peering at Birrick through a pair of cracked glasses.

"You would be doing me a favour."

"Yes, and why should I? Elves, bah!" The hermit stroked his chin, waiting to hear Birrick's reply.

"But I must not fail, I have the key. The rose is only for the pure-hearted. How can you deny me? I need to get back to the Other World!"

"Yes, and I'd like to go to Majorca for a beach holiday, or even to the Isle of Man, but I'm here. You need a really good reason to convince me. Try harder."

A voice, Mr Unreal, whispered to Birrick, "The medal fool." Birrick touched the medal and felt a tingling sensation in his fingers.

"In the name of the angels, the goblins, the shapeshifters, the Seer, I call on you to give me passage, or you will be left to sit here for another five hundred years, with no holiday, and no dog to talk to, and no name." Birrick gulped at his cheek.

"And if I let you through?"

"I will let you know your name, and I will cure your dog of his choking fit and bad temper, perhaps then you'll get a holiday."

"Try then," said the hermit.

Birrick turned, pointing his key at the dog, "Canus voluit et canus bibit ex flumina est vita."

The dog let out a long blood-curdling howl, crawled to the river, and drank thirstily. Turning to the hermit, the dog trotted up beside him and licked the hermit's feet.

"So, what's my name, elf?" asked the hermit.

"Tolcan," replied Birrick. "Tolcan, let me through." The dog raised his head, and the crack in the rocks parted, to reveal a secret passage. The hermit patted his dog and beckoned to Birrick.

"You will find the way, but will the way find you?" The hermit smiled and nodded to Birrick.

Hurrying forward, Birrick manoeuvred past the hermit and through the gap in the rocks. Going forward, something brushed Birrick's left ear.

"Hello, can I join you?" whispered a soft voice. A bat with a human face had perched on Birrick's shoulder.

Birrick could see what looked like several spiders, skeletons, and large beetles in among the rocks as he tried to pass through. Then Birrick paused, he thought he could hear another noise, though he could not identify what it was, a soft pad. Coming around a particularly big donkey-shaped rock, Birrick could see a very large rat, with whiskers, a long tail, and baring sharp teeth. Saliva dripped from its mouth as it crouched, hissing, then rearing up on its hind legs, flicking its tail.

The bat flew at the rat, digging its fangs into the rat's neck. As the bat sucked, it grew bigger, and the rat squeaked, shrinking, getting ever smaller. Eventually, reduced to the size of a small pet, the rat ran off. The bat however turned into the dark-haired, dark-clothed Dracul, who stood there brushing cobwebs out of his hair. "Come with me," said Dracul in a low voice. Dracul held up a pointed long-handled knife, which glowed a red colour, giving off a strange light. Relieved, Birrick followed Dracul through the rocky passage, until they came to a curtain of blood-red satin which hid whatever lay behind.

Swiftly, Dracul took Birrick by the hand, while trying to push him through the curtain. Stepping through the curtain, the ground fell away beneath Birrick, he could not find any hold in the sheer steep rock. He was dangling over the precipice of a gorge, clinging on with one hand to Dracul.

"Give it to me, give me the rose and I will save you elf." Dracul held onto Birrick firmly. Looking down, Birrick could see a steep drop, looking up, he looked into Dracul's piercing eyes. Birrick wanted to scream with fear.

"Never," cried Birrick, "never, I believe in the angels, the goblins, the elves. Dracul, you drink blood, you will not drink mine, 'con nostra sanguine bibire, con vos sanguine mendax et bibit, furcifer'."

Losing his grip on Birrick, the Dracul let him go. Slipping and sliding down the bank of the gorge, Birrick tumbled into the Wizard's Well. Falling, spiralling downwards, Birrick's short life flashed before his eyes. Reaching the bottom, he lay there, dazed, and scratched. Looking around, there was an oval mirror, in which Birrick could see the Seer. The Seer held out his hand, and he took it, stepping through the mirror into the Seer's secret chamber, another place of magic and hiding. What would lie in store next?

Chapter Seven

Birrick stepped through the mirror and went down on bended knee before the Seer.

"I have the rose, oh wise one," gulped Birrick, handing it over to the Seer.

The Seer took the rose. Promptly it grew a long stem, branches, and roots.

"Ahh yes, it is the everlasting rose after all," said the Seer; he potted it in a small purple plant pot at the side of his mirror, where immediately many white flowers began to bloom from the branches.

"Now Birrick," said the Seer. "It's not over yet."

"But I have the rose for you, it's not fair," wailed Birrick.

"However, friend, you do not yet have the stone of second sight, do you?" The Seer looked at Birrick seriously.

"Aren't you going to give it to me now?"

"No."

"Oh, why?"

"I don't have it here. I will give you a companion to journey with you. He will take you to the quarry of the worm where the most precious stones can be found. You will be protected. Here, Crimthain, Crimthain Volpus." the Seer beckoned, and a wolf-like dog, covered in grey fur leapt through the mirror, landing at the Seer's feet.

"Crimthain, you will take Birrick to the place of the worm. Then, when he returns safely with the stone he seeks, I will put a charm on it, so that it will give second sight and knowledge of the secrets of the Other World. You will not fail Crimthain. Dracul will not bother you for a while."

"What is this worm?" Birrick asked, hesitantly.

"The worm is a strange, dark slippery creature. It breathes fire. It has a deathly bite, and strong senses; it can sense sound, presence, smell, touch. It can't see, it doesn't need to. For this animal, the senses are very acute. It lies most of its time curled in a quarry, sometimes venturing to eat sheep or children, or maybe elves. Mostly, however, the worm sleeps. The quarry has been left unworked for many years since the worm took up home there. The trick is to outwit the worm."

"And how big is this worm?"

"Oh, about thirty feet long, three feet wide, with a gaping mouth. If it breathes on you, then you could burn to death."

Birrick frowned, "Is there any other way to get the stone?"

"No, just that," the Seer smiled. "You seem worried?"

"Only, surprised. Where is this quarry?"

"On the other side of the Jagged Edge, beyond the Layered Mountains. Near the source of the Moon's river, and the Wendish stone circle."

"But that's miles away!"

"Birrick, put your elfin thinking cap on, you will have Crimthain, you can use elf magic. It is not so far. You must try in order to succeed."

"But how?"

"Take Crimthain as your guide, you can ride on his back, a puny elf like you, he will carry you with ease."

The Seer waved his right arm, chanting, "Vulpus voluit, vulpus voluit."

The wolf howled, then rubbed itself against Birrick.

"Crimthain, no eating young maidens, and be helpful to Birrick our friend. Get on his back Birrick."

Birrick tried and fell off.

"Do you have a rein that I could hold onto?" Birrick looked hopefully at the Seer.

"You are a novice aren't you? Very well," the old seer pointed his finger at Crimthain. "Apparatus harness," he said. A rein immediately appeared with a harness around the wolf's neck. The wolf blinked, growled at Birrick, daring him to try again.

"Go on." The Seer waved at them. "Go on."

Birrick got onto the wolf and held the reins. "Vamos vulpus," cried Birrick. Crimthain leapt through the mirror, and there they were, out in a cold icy landscape, the Layered Mountains, with many tall peaks topped with snow. A bird called, it was an owl, suddenly flying low in front of them. Then a stone whizzed past, barely missing them. A large footprint appeared in front, in the snow, then another and another. Sitting on a boulder, a strange, hunched figure, like a large man, was throwing pebbles, stones, and bones.

"Wait, you there, what's the password?" The ogre demanded angrily, "What's the password, without permission you cannot enter the pass of the ogre or go any further. What is it?"

"Who is asking?" replied Birrick.

"I am asking you, me, the Ogre of the Mountains. If you take one more step without pleasing me, I will turn you into a baked potato and eat you. Ha!"

Birrick screwed up his elfin forehead and touched the medal still at his neck. "The password is 'exitus vulpus'," shouted Birrick, loudly. "Exitus vulpus, Crimthain venga, vamos."

"No," said the ogre. "No, try again."

"Er, abracadabra?" asked Birrick.

"No, and this is your last go," said the ogre, rubbing his hands.

"Ingang, ootgang, hollowbone, noot man." queried Birrick. He could hear a tone of desperation in his voice.

"Alright," said the ogre. "It's the way, go past. I like a bit of Geordie, not all that fancy stuff."

Crimthain trotted past the ogre, Birrick held onto the reins, and again the owl hooted ahead. It was getting dark; the moon was visible in the sky. Crimthain turned to eye Birrick, then snorted, pausing to drink from the snow on the ground.

A screeching wail carried on the night air, in the eerie light of the moon, the bird called again. Birrick felt a shadow pass him. There, perched on Crimthain's head was an eagle. The bird tilted its head on one side, suddenly it lunged at Birrick. He put his hand to his face in defence, but the bird of prey kept pecking at him, lunging at his arm, face, and hair. "Caw caw," cried out the bird. Taking off in flight it tried to dig its talons into Birrick's back. "Run Crimthain, run," shouted Birrick in fright. The wolf picked up speed, but the eagle flew beside them. The path over which they ran followed around a tarn. Crimthain leapt into the icy water. Birrick chilled already in the night air, felt the water seep through his clothes, into his

55

shoes, and trousers. As Crimthain ploughed on, the water came up to Birrick's neck. The eagle called out 'caw caw' and it almost sounded to Birrick as if the bird was screeching out 'how unfair'. Altering its flight, the eagle swooped in another, more westerly direction, and disappeared. The dark water around Birrick seemed threatening. Seeing a fire burning beside a bothie at the near side of the tarn, the wolf paddled into the shallows, then mounted a grassy bank.

"Hello," said a man with a short ginger beard. He sat beside the fire, roasting meat, and potatoes.

"Hungry elf?" the man asked, his clothing and gun at his side indicated a hunter or gamekeeper.

"Go on," said the ginger bearded man. A blonde boy with a scar on his cheek took a knife and carved some venison pieces off, giving them to Birrick. The meat was hot to touch, Birrick dropped it. Dismounting Crimthain, Birrick took off the reins. The wolf immediately bent to taste the meat, eating what he could.

The man and boy, sitting by the fire smiled. "We're from around here. This is my nephew Jake." The ginger bearded man drank from a flask. "Why are you here? Where are you journeying?" Looking pointedly at Birrick, the man said, "I'm Red, we don't see many elves around here. Perhaps you can give me a charm in return for a safe night. I need some magic; elf magic could be alright."

"Why do you need magic?" Birrick asked.

"I need a way to make a woman love me."

"Which woman?"

"My wife."

"Why did she stop loving you?"

"I don't think she ever did, or maybe only at first. Some druids came to the village, one taught her how to tell fortunes. Then she threatened to tell my fortune and said that she could ruin me."

"She has cursed you?"

"Yes, I suppose so, and we have no children. I take back meat, I grow crops, but she won't come near me."

Birrick sat looking into the fire. "You need a love spell."

"Yes, can you give me one?"

Birrick looked straight at the man, gazing into the hardened face and sad brown eyes.

"Take four leaves. Write on them in red ink your wife's name, and put one leaf in every corner of your bedroom, under the carpet. Burn a red candle, before the next full moon, in your bedroom, and let it burn out. Take a red paper heart shape, write on it in red ink your heart's desire, and put it in the pocket over your heart. At the next full moon, take the heart and the leaves, burn them, with a corn dolly, all wrapped in a pink silk scarf. Bury the ashes close to your home, in your garden if you have one. Pour out a mead libation to the pink lady over the burial spot."

"The pink lady?" asked Red.

"A well-known spirit who helps in cases of a wounded heart," replied Birrick.

"Thanks, elf," said Red. "Would you like to share our bothie tonight?" Red gestured to the stone building behind them.

"No thank you, soon we will have to continue. But perhaps you could give me some food and drink? A small meal? Crimthain ate the meat, it was too hot for me. I would like a potato and a brew of tea if you're making some." Birrick cheered up at the look on Red's face.

"Fine," said Red. "I can fix that, no problem. Jake, get the kettle out of the bothie with the necessary, we'll make a brew to go with these roasted potatoes." Jake got up to go inside, and Red stroked his face, looking at Birrick. "You still haven't said why you're here?"

"There is a reason," said Birrick. "It involves a woman."

"Then say no more, even I know how women can be unreasonable." Red poked at the fire and placed the kettle which Jake handed him over the flames.

Red started to whistle, then pulled two hot potatoes wrapped in foil out of the campfire. He handed these to Birrick.

"Tuck in, the brew will be ready soon, and you'll be on your way. All because of a woman, eh? Women, yes, and how we need them, and how it hurts me when my wife won't do as I wish. She spends too much time looking at the tea leaves. Calls herself a hedge witch, she even took a new name, Ally Arundel, and brought in a stray cat, which she calls Gomorrah. Why couldn't she be happy without magic?" Red looked at Birrick sadly.

"Well, people are always looking for something more, or something else. Magic is that, for a lot of us."

"And through this what?" Red asked.

"Through this a way to achieve our dreams or gain insight. Perhaps some of us even look for power through magic, power over others."

"Or power to reincarnate? My wife thinks that she is a reincarnation of Salome. She wants revenge, revenge on men."

"Try the charm that I told you, it could work, and remember, tell no one about this. For it to be a powerful charm, you must keep it a secret. Those charms are only to be handed down to those in genuine need. I genuinely needed the potato, so there you go."

The kettle started to boil, steam coming out of the spout.

"Tea, here." Red made the brew and passed a hot mug to Birrick. "I don't know many elves, I'll have to take your word if you're soon going off."

Birrick looked at the position of the moon and drained his mug. Crimthain was lying curled up on the other side of the fire, enjoying the flames.

"Crimthain," called Birrick, "vulpus venga." The wolf trotted up to Birrick and licked him on the cheek.

"Uuuurgh!" said Birrick, wiping his face, then standing up, and mounting Crimthain the wolf companion. "Vulpus vamos!" shouted Birrick, holding tightly onto the reins. In seconds they left the bothie and Red behind them, continuing to journey true north.

Passing mountain after mountain, they journeyed along the narrow twisting path. Travelling in the night, the goblin's medal hung at Birrick's neck, giving a kind of comfort. Whenever Birrick looked at the key, it glowed brightly. Now and then, Birrick rubbed the medal and felt a sense of purpose. As they turned around a winding precipice edge, the path forked. Looking down, Birrick felt dizzy. He patted Crimthain so that the wolf stopped. Peering down the mountainside, Birrick realized that he was looking over a series of ledges, set in a mountain face. At the bottom, far, far beneath, lay the curled form of a large curious worm. A bluish-white light, coming from around the worm, reflecting in a scintillating fashion, indicated many precious or semi-precious stones. This, Birrick realized, was the Jagged Edge, below which slept the terrible worm. Occasionally the worm would breathe fire as it slept, lighting up the hoard of stones.

Birrick patted Crimthain again, "First to the Wendish Stone Circle, so that I can prepare for my last task." With that, Birrick and Crimthain took the right fork in the path, journeying up, and west over the mountain instead of down.

They were travelling against the prevailing wind. Birrick felt fresh with the spirit of adventure still alive in him, and the thought of the Other World, to which he hoped to return. Crossing over the mountain top, a view of moorland thick with heather, and a circle of ten standing stones.

"Hurry Crimthain, hurry," whispered Birrick to the wolf. Rising to the challenge, Crimthain raced through the night in the direction of the ancient standing stones. The Wendish Stones surrounded a spring of fresh water which had been blessed by Hilda the Wendish Hag. Brushing through the moorland, and running into the stone circle, Birrick could hear the trickle of running water. Dismounting Crimthain, and stooping to drink from the spring, which welled up at the base of a stone cairn. Birrick felt a surge of energy. Drawing a magic circle around himself and the wolf, many photons of light began to gather above the cairn, in the centre of the stones. Picking up a small rock, he ran widdershins around the inner side of the stone ring then returning to the cairn, he placed the rock at its base. The photon glow increased, taking the shape of a large green eye, which blinked. Birrick drew the symbol of infinity in the night air, gazing up at the green eye. Birrick cupped his hands, took some water from the spring, dousing Crimthain, then himself. The eye blinked again and was gone. Birrick, alongside his wolf friend, was alone in the deepening darkness. Holding up the key, he was dazzled by the light it shed. Lifting it high, Birrick started to chant, "Now faith and hope go with me, lead me on to victory, stay by me, and keep me whole, guide me on until I'm home." Putting it back in his pocket, Birrick turned to mount Crimthain. Then he heard a whispering in the night, not just the wind, it was Mr Unreal, "Hurry Birrick, Dracul wants the stones, Dracul wants the key. Dracul has been following you. The forces of darkness are with Dracul, not you. Hurry, hurry, you are not home yet." Birrick paused and dipped his index finger in the spring. Making the sign of a star on his forehead, he bowed low to the spirit there. Crimthain the wolf drank from the spring, then the two left together, on leaving Birrick looked back over his left shoulder; a blue star hung there in the sky, low down, near the horizon. With the wind behind them, Birrick whooped, and they ran on, hoping for better ahead.

Chapter Eight

Not long had passed when the two wanderers came to a knotted tree, bent with the wind. The tree hung in the darkness over the Jagged Edge, seemingly clinging to the earth; roots visible, branches bare. Birrick reined in Crimthain, giving a signal to stop. Pressing his finger to his lips, Birrick whispered to the wolf, "Stay here until I return. No howling or whining please.",

Feeling brave, and with high hopes, Birrick left his friend the wolf and started down the shale track which led to the quarry below. Taking out the key, which gave a silvery light, Birrick could see several birds nesting on ledges in the quarry walls. The track led down a steep bank so that Birrick clutched at roots or prickly branches on his way down. Sometimes stumbling, but always quiet, Birrick made as little noise as possible. While at the edge of the quarry Birrick felt the cold night air, the further down he stumbled, the warmer he became. The heat coming from the worm, and its size, surprised Birrick. The occasional snort of fiery breath which the worm gave out as it slept, lit up the darkness. Though the worm was coiled, Birrick could tell that it was a dull silvery grey colour, with small legs. Unlike a dragon, the worm had no wings but still looked unpleasant in its slumbering state. Birrick did not doubt that it might give a nasty bite.

The many stones which littered the quarry floor reflected a beautiful rainbow of colours like stained glass. Birrick could see the stones he wanted, giving off a lovely pale blue moonlike shine. The snag is that these iridescent bluish stones are nearest to the worm's tail end. Birrick rubbed his medal and holding his key aloft, he tiptoed over pebbles and grass towards the bluish stones. The worm moved, rolled over, and snorted. Birrick held his breath waiting. Nothing happened, the worm still slept. Manoeuvring carefully by walking slowly, quietly around the worm, Birrick stretched out his hand, to touch the stones. Picking three stones from the hoard, Birrick's fingers closed around the smooth blue crystals, and he put them in his pouch. Turning, and keeping his eyes on the worm, Birrick began to move off, up and along the quarry track.

He struggled up the assent, found it difficult, and the path, steep. A woman with golden hair in a white robe appeared before him. She held out a bow and arrows.

"Take this Birrick," she said. "You will do good. I wish you luck." As she disappeared, Birrick caught a faint smell of roses. Climbing further and putting his feet on the scree, he bent to clutch at a root and stumbled. A small avalanche of scree pebbles made a noise. It wasn't much, but it sounded loud in the quiet of the night. As the pebbles rolled down into the quarry, a large, pointed pebble hit the worm on its head. Raising its horrible, segmented body, and breathing a foul, fiery, sulphuric breath, the worm reared up. A shot of fire scorched the track, burning the laces in Birrick's shoes.

Putting an arrow to the bow, Birrick turned his aim at the worm. One arrow hit the worm in its body. The worm screamed, breathing out more fire. The next arrow shot was a complete miss. Taking aim again, and saying a quiet blessing on the place, Birrick shot his final arrow. This time the arrow lodged itself in the worm's head. It writhed, coiled, uncoiled, and rolled on the quarry floor. Birrick ran up the track as quickly as he could. At the top, he could see Crimthain waiting. Dropping the bow, Birrick scrambled up the last of the uneven route. Climbing onto Crimthain's back, the elf and the wolf friend disappeared into the dark.

As the two friends journeyed on, Birrick noticed a certain uneven limping when Crimthain ran. Coming around the mountainside of the Jagged Edge, Crimthain detoured from the path, coming to rest at a cavern opening in the rocky scree. Birrick kneed Crimthain, and Crimthain lay down, licking his front left paw, there was blood. Birrick knew that Crimthain was hurt. Taking a closer look at his friend, Birrick could see a thorn in Crimthain's paw. He bent down, took the paw, and spat out the grass, dirt, and blood in Crimthain's toes as he gripped his elfin teeth around the thorn and pulled. Taking out the thorn and looking at it closely, Birrick noticed that it had a golden point. "Strange," he murmured, putting the thorn in his pouch with the stones. Crimthain rested his head on the cave floor. "Come on Crimthain," said Birrick. "We have to go." But Crimthain turned his head in the direction of the cavernous deep as if to say, "It's alright for you in there." He closed his eyes as if to sleep. "Crimthain, vamos!" cried Birrick. Crimthain ignored him and let out a sigh. A ray of sunlight from the horizon lit up the cavern. Birrick watched the sunrise, and then looked again at Crimthain. The wolf had turned completely white, except for a greyish nose and tail. Birrick patted his friend, he was stiff and cold. There was no movement, only silence. Stroking the fur of his wolf-friend, Birrick knew that Crimthain was dead.

Looking around at the walls of the cavern, Birrick could see various pentacles and strange spirals drawn on the walls. He heard the sound of rushing water coming from deep inside the mountain. Drawn onwards by a magnetic pull, he wandered on, holding up the silvery luminous key as a light in the dank dark.

Going further into the bowels of the cavern, the sound of rushing water grew louder, until it became a thundering torrent at Birrick's feet. The underground river was too wide even for an elf to jump. Several rocks or stones were protruding in the river's surface, and he thought that he might be able to use these as steppingstones. The stones looked green with algae, the waters seemed deep, strong, with a powerful current in the dark waters. Gingerly putting a foot on the first stone, Birrick could see his mother, waving to him, on the other side. Filled with longing and loneliness, Birrick jumped onto the next rock. A rope swung suddenly in front of him, and he grasped at it to steady himself, intending to swing over to the next stone in his reach. His hands closed around the rope, and with a jolt, the rope swung upwards, giving him a mild electric shock. The rope pulled him, instead of him pulling the rope. As he rose into the damp air, a head appeared on the end of what looked like more rope. The head was a snake head, hissing, and spitting. Looking at the small evil eyes of the snake head, seven similar snakeheads swung around him. The heads spat at Birrick, hoping for a fresh victim. Terrified, Birrick let go of his grasp of the rope and fell into the waters of the underground river. A man with tattoos stamped a large wooden staff on the other side, and the ropes, snake heads, and hissing were gone.

Swallowing large amounts of water, Birrick, an elf who could not swim, tried to float. As he floated, he collided with a large rock in the water. Flailing, he started to lose consciousness and go under. The river was claiming him, all he could hear was the rushing of the water in his ears, and all he could see was dark water sparkling with stars.

Feeling something soft under his head, Birrick opened his eyes. He was lying on a sandbank, where the river current had left him. Three tall thin women towered over him. A woman with red hair, a pointed white face, dressed in many multi-coloured pearls poked him in the ribs.

"Get off," said Birrick.

"Then why don't you get up?" the woman replied. "I am the Rowan Witch, Queen of the Underworld. These are my sisters, the Hazel Witch and the Yew Witch. What quest are you on? Why are you here in our time? Don't you belong somewhere, elf?"

Birrick swallowed hard wondering what to say. He sat up slowly and his back hurt. He noticed that the women all wore long dark dresses. One witch had black hair, the other silver with many silver ornaments around her neck and bells on her dress.

"I…I er…am on my way to…er… the Wizard's Well. A strong undercurrent dragged me here."

Birrick put his hand in his pocket where he hoped to find the key.

"You're trespassing elf," said the Rowan witch, "come with us, you could be useful."

Birrick's pocket was empty, with no key. All his fingers could detect was the thorn from Crimthain's paw. Feeling scared he stood up. He was much shorter than the witches. The Yew witch took him by the arm, got on her yew broom, and dangled Birrick along in a black cloth sack. Flying in formation, each witch on her broomstick, they flew off along the course of the river.

"But I have to go home," wailed Birrick out loud.

"It's no use complaining. You should have thought of that before." The Hazel witch laughed a bell-like laugh, and in the air tunnel, the silver bells on her dress tinkled in a strange unearthly jangled tune.

The three witches flew on the brooms through an open window into a large underground kitchen. The Hazel witch flung Birrick into a corner of the kitchen, where he collided with a wooden dresser. A white cat with a human face meowed at him. There was a large cauldron, bubbling in a hearth over the open fire. On a black granite plinth, resting on a trestle table, was a much larger than usual quartz crystal ball. The witches sang in unison, standing at the fire.

"Feed him fishes, clean the dishes, turtle soup, and black beetroot.

Round our pot, we scheme a lot.

We frighten elves, magic's afoot.

Let's down the broth and be uncouth!"

With that, each witch dipped a bowl into the cauldron and swigged their fill. Birrick sat there, dazed, feeling alone, and even wishing he was back in Malloway. Creeping over to the table, he stared into the crystal ball. Whilst staring, he felt drawn in, something sucking his attention. He could not avert his gaze. Finally, he could see the garden of Malloway House, the pond, the garden seat, the treehouse where he often swung on the rope ladder. The Yew witch smiled at him, showing bad black teeth. She offered him a bowl of stew, and he accepted. Tasting a little, the food made him feel warm inside so that he quickly downed it and asked for more. The Yew witch grinned again and shook her head at him. The three witches turned their full attention on Birrick and the ball. Birrick shuddered, the vision in the ball vanished. Instead, a man with tattoos stared at him from the crystal, blinked then disappeared. Birrick wondered how he could escape this time. He sensed that the witches would offer no real help; he could not find the key, and they were stronger in numbers, more powerful than he was. After all, he was only a lone elf.

Chapter Nine

As the days passed, and life in the kitchen fell into a routine of cleaning, carrying, feeding, sleeping, Birrick was aware that his place was as a servant, a scullery do-it-all elf. Not only did Birrick have the care of the kitchen, polishing various spoons, cauldrons, assorted crystal balls, he also had a duty to feed several peculiar creatures kept by the witches. In one kitchen cupboard, there was a large glass bottle, larger than a man. It contained a woman who had sharp teeth, webbed hands, and feet. Birrick had to throw bread and scones into the narrow bottleneck, through which the woman could not escape. In another cupboard was a cage, in which sat what looked like a large hairy ape-man. The ape growled, spoke little English, and took cakes or bananas when offered. One night, when the witches were sitting around the fire, Birrick said, "What are the names of these creatures, why do you keep them?"

The Yew witch smiled at this and said, "We have others, you have not seen all our grotesques yet. They are spells gone wrong; we keep them because it entertains us. We brought them into existence through magic. The woman is Ariel, the ape, Caliban. Here is another of our mistakes, follow me."

The Yew witch took Birrick to another cupboard. Here, a large stripey ginger cat with a man's head slept upon a velvet cushion. "Sometimes the spells go wrong, so we keep our pets. Hazel!" called out Yew. "What happened to the other mistake, the seven-headed snake?"

"I think we let it loose in the river," replied Hazel. "Rowan, what time is our next witching hour?"

"Two hours ahead," replied Rowan. "We need to patrol the Underworld for a while first. You, Birrick, may also be here because of a spell that went wrong. You didn't think of that, did you?"

The witches laughed in a horrible cackle, like geese. "You could make a nice elf stew," said Yew. The witch looked at Birrick with dilated dark eyes, the pupil covering the whole iris.

"Look after our kitchen Birrick," said Rowan. "We will be gone for a while."

The three sisters mounted their brooms flying up and out a narrow staircase.

Birrick shivered. The cat with a man's head strolled out of its hideaway over to Birrick, gazing at him quietly.

"I've heard it all before," said the cat. "My name is Mr Cheese; how do you do?"

"What do they mean?" asked Birrick.

"If you do not know, then I shall not say. What do you want?"

"To find a way out of here."

"Then I have something you will need. I ate this along with a fish." The cat started coughing and spluttering. Then out of its mouth came a fish head landing on the floor at Birrick's feet.

70

"Look closely," said the cat man. "It's been causing me indigestion." In the fish's mouth was the head of a silver key.

Birrick picked up the green fish head, and carefully pulled out the key. With a flood of hope, his toenails tingling, Birrick recognized the silver key from the Well of Melancholy. The key which he had lost in the river.

"Keep it," said the cat. "you need it to get out of here. Back to the Wizard's Well, huh? And where is your companion?"

"Companion?" replied Birrick.

"The wolf. We saw him in the crystal ball, you and him before you came here."

"I don't know where Crimthain is now. He turned white, and I thought he would take me back to the Well. Only Crimthain died, so I am here, and I need to escape this place."

"There is a way," said Mr Cheese, "but it is not without danger. You still need to cross the river which nearly drowned you. You fell in, as so many do, which is how they get their servants."

"So, how can I cross? How can I escape? Tell me."

"First," said the Cat, "get me a drink of milk."

Immediately, Birrick ran to the larder, where there was a large blue jug of good milk. Taking it and placing it in front of the man-cat, he waited to see what would happen.

The man-cat put his paw into the jug, licked it, then put his head into the jug, making loud slurping sounds. Pausing, the man-cat lifted his head to think. "Now Birrick, look back. When you were with Crimthain, did you remove something from his paw? Something with a golden tip?"

"Yes, a thorn."

"You have this with you, in a pocket or a purse?" The man-cat looked at him, his eyes blue with flecks of grey.

"Let me see," said Birrick, putting his hands into the pockets of his jacket. Nothing. Then under the jacket, Birrick felt his purse pouch. Pulling it out, he opened it. Inside were three moonstones and a golden-tipped thorn. Birrick took out the thorn, showing it to the cat.

"Yes, that's it. It's from the Myriad Tree. From this tree, with the right spell, many myriad possibilities open. Toss this thorn onto the banks of the river, say the right magic words, you will find your way."

"How?"

"Try," said the cat-man. "Just try."

"But what are the right words?"

"You will know." The cat-man smiled an inscrutable smile, then returned to the cushion, curled up, and went to sleep.

Birrick looked at the thorn lying in the palm of his hand. Feeling a mounting wish to escape the witches' kitchen, he rubbed the coin at his neck. Holding the key up to his face, he concentrated. The key slowly began to glow, and Birrick felt a magnetic pull. Saying out loud, "Credo", Birrick let the key guide him. Climbing out of the kitchen window, he sneaked out and found his way to the riverside.

There on the mossy, earthy bank, Birrick bent to kiss the earth, and pressed the thorn, gold tip pointing downwards, into it. Screwing up his forehead in a frown, he whispered out aloud.

"Arbus maximus, supra flumen mea porta." Closing his eyes and counting to ten, Birrick waited to see the result.

Something scratched him in the face, Birrick opened his eyes to see. Before him a tree was growing, in an arch, with a twisted trunk, growing over the river. The tree had many curving tendrils, one had hit Birrick in the face. The stem of the tree looked strong enough to carry an elf. Letting out a long sigh, Birrick whispered, "Very well then, I believe."

The sound of rushing water was loud in Birrick's ears. He wondered whether to crawl up the trunk and across the river or to swing using the tendrils. He took hold of one of the curling fronds and pulled. It broke off in his hands. So, straddling the trunk, Birrick managed to pull himself along with his hands, pushing with his legs and knees. Looking up into the high cavern, Birrick could only see shadows and darkness. Following his instincts, he inched his way along the tree. Trying to look down, the speed of the water and his height made him feel dizzy. Nearing the other side, he reached for a vine tendril. He missed and lurched to one side. Leaning close to the trunk to steady himself, he closed his eyes for a second. In the darkness, he heard the voice of Mr Unreal, "Go on, you will fall otherwise." Struggling to an upright standing position, Birrick walked the last measure of the tree and jumped with one almighty leap. Landing on the damp earth, he heard the voice again, "Turn and see." Looking back, the tree was receding, twisting back into its base, and eventually, there was no trace of foliage or tendrils, simply a stump in the ground.

"Quick," said Mr Unreal. "Go quickly. Soon the witches will be searching for you." Birrick put his hand on the key, it pulled him with magnetic power, into darkness. Birrick hoped that it would lead him to the Seer.

Veering off down a tunnel, Birrick heard an echoing cackle that scared him. Running until it hurt, he heard the crackle of laughter again, nearer and scarier. "Birrick," called Yew's voice. "Birrick, I am watching you. You cannot escape." Then more laughter, and a blackbird – or was it a bat– flew past him. He felt fear churning in his stomach. Running as fast as he could, in semi-darkness, he could see a dim light ahead. In front of him, a vague figure in silver began to materialize in a silvery dress; Rowan.

"You will never escape, Birrick. You are ours, you belong to us." Rowan stretched out her arms, they grew, and all around her grew a large silver cobweb that covered the passage. Birrick held the key aloft, as he reached the cobweb he slashed it with his key and continued running.

"It's useless to try Birrick," called Yew. "You are ours."

"You can never survive here without us," shrieked Hazel.

Birrick, however, kept running from the weird sisters. A further light, strong and gold, drew him on. With all his might hurtling forwards, beads of cold sweat on his brow, Birrick was suddenly standing in the light. There was the mirror, the seer on the other side, and a hand holding out to pull him on. Jumping through, he fell to the floor, collapsed in a heap of sweat and tears.

"There," said the Seer. "Look," the Seer pointed at the mirror; there was Rowan, banging her fists on the glass. She picked up a stone and threw it at the mirror. It bounced back, hitting her in the face, and fixing itself in her right eye socket. Screaming out in pain, she turned to float up the passage, taking her cobwebs with her, cursing as she left.

Chapter Ten

"You still have the key?" asked the Seer.

"Yes, though at one point, I thought it was lost."

"And the stones?" queried the old wizard?

"Here." Birrick held out his pouch containing the moonstones. Opening his purse pouch, he emptied its contents onto the Seer's velvet footstool. They glowed with a slight bluish silver light. Birrick heard and felt faint vibrations of music and a harp singing.

"Congratulations! With these, I will give you the gift you need. We must go together to a special place, to make the necessary magic. What became of Crimthain?"

Birrick looked at the floor, saddened. "Crimthain turned whiter and whiter until he died. There was a thorn in his paw, though I am not sure whether that killed him."

"It may have been poisoned Birrick. Did it have a gold tip?"

"Yes."

"Then probably that killed him, the particular type of magic in such a thorn can be poisonous. Now, we must be on our way, the Blind Guardian will help us."

"Where are we going?"

"Come with me, I will show you now," said the Seer. Picking up his purple cloak which had been lying on the chair, the Seer wrapped it around himself. "We are going to the Darkening Castle."

"Haven't I already been?" asked Birrick.

"No, not to this part you haven't. Pick up your stones and follow me." The Seer led the way, through the underground network of passages, coming eventually to a large stone that blocked the way.

"Do you know how these passages were made Birrick?"

"No."

"They were made by miners, some of whom lost their lives down here. They were digging for coal, which made this part of the world a hive of business. In some ways, the black coal was as precious as diamonds. Point the key at the stone."

Birrick held up the silver key and did as he was told. A sound like thunder could be heard, then there was bright magnesium like flash. The stone rolled to one side, revealing a dark dungeon. There was a statue at the centre of the underground room. Birrick blinked, he thought he had seen the statue before. The statue revolved, then walked, and Birrick knew that this was the golden-haired guardian who had come to help him.

"Birrick," the golden-haired woman said softly. "Birrick, you have the gift of good fortune. You are here in time. Show me the stones."

Birrick carefully got out the stones which were still glowing with a peculiar light.

"Now we must go out, into the night, we will weave our spell, and follow the light. We must leave the dungeon of Darkworth, stepping into the shining of the moon." The golden-haired woman led the way, with the one eye open in her forehead. She sang in a peculiar high-pitched voice, a voice that sounded like moon motes. They climbed the dank steps of the dungeon, walking out of the castle door into the night air.

Proceeding down the wooden outer staircase, the three trod the grass of the castle square, within the castle walls. Stopping near the well, the golden-haired guardian held up her hand as a signal to the others. "My other name is Nemesis," she said. "I am here to see that only those who deserve a good fate, get one. You have acted with a good heart, so you bring good on yourself. Now Birrick, put the moonstones on this rock, here in the light of this shining night. No harm will come."

Birrick did as the Guardian indicated.

Dancing around the stones, the Guardian, Birrick, and the Seer chanted,

"We three. We three. A gift for thee. A gift of sight. A gift that's bright, in this moonlight, gives second sight. A secret dream, no need to scheme, the right gift gives the second sight. Now to this world, we give the light." Putting their hands together over the stones, the Guardian spoke to the other two,

"It is done, soon I will be gone. Use your time wisely."

Floating off in a cloud of gold, she left the Seer and Birrick standing on the grass. "Where has she gone?" asked Birrick. "There is one other thing that I need."

"Now you ask me?" queried the Seer, raising his eyebrows.

"I need to know the secrets of the Other World."

"Well, to merit this, you must find the Mean Miser, and pay him." The Seer laughed. "You need too much Birrick, and everything will come to you, in good time. You cannot put the Other World, with all it holds, into a bottle or a recipe. These things are simply revealed, at the right time, in the right way. Some things are faith or a state of mind Birrick. You believe, as I do, in magic. It is believing at the end, which affects your mind making magic work. This is what leads to proof or revelation."

Birrick looked sadly at the Seer. "And now?"

"You must meet the Mean Miser and go with him and his friends to Malloway House. He will be waiting for you. From there, you will find the way. Sally will be pleased with you, but there may be more for you to do."

"More?" Birrick looked at him aghast.

"Yes friend, there may be more. Now go with my blessing." With this, the Seer made the sign of the star and climbed down into the castle well. As he disappeared into the world below, the Seer waved, calling out, "Farewell Birrick, safe journeying comes with a sacrifice. On your way."

The last Birrick could see of the Seer was his greyish hair, and then nothing. Only silence and the sounds of the night.

Birrick stood, nonplussed for a few seconds. Then he started to look for a way out of the castle square. The walls were high, the gate was locked, but as he looked at the walls, there seemed to be a rough stone staircase which he might be able to climb up to get over the top. The walls were built on a steep bank. As Birrick climbed the stairs he grasped at various ledges and grazed his knee. Reaching the heights of the walls, and looking over, he wondered where he could safely jump. Walking along the top of the wall, sometimes crawling, he came to the main gate where there seemed to be a safe enough landing place. Focusing his eyes on the spot he was intending to land on, Birrick leapt with all his youthful might, shouting out, "Venga, vene, vidi, vici." As he somersaulted, his short elfin life passed before his eyes. He fell to earth, landing on his feet like a gymnast.

Walking into the village of Darkworth, Birrick came to a bus stop. Looking at the timetable, he realized that there would be no busses for several hours. Disappointed, he walked on, down an old high street full of quaint cottages, old pubs, and craft shops. Eventually, he came to a churchyard. Elves are normally superstitious, but Birrick wondered whether he should sleep there, as he felt rather tired. There would be little traffic at this time, so no hope of a lift home. Investigating the churchyard grounds further, Birrick found a spot where the grass seemed softer, and the area more sheltered by the church side. Lying down despite the cold north wind, he pulled his jacket around him, intending to sleep.

After a few minutes, Birrick started to snore, rhythmically. The presence of a snoring elf in the graveyard disturbed the restless spirits, who one by one gathered around him to peer at the spectacle. A whole host of ghouls hovered over Birrick's sleeping body. Birrick started to dream, and in his sleeping state, a shadowy spirit said to Birrick, "What are you doing in our graveyard? Are you going to take us home with you?"

The spirits, which had not passed over, danced around Birrick in his dream state. Rolling over, he knocked a gravestone, which gave him a cold, sharp shock. Opening his eyes in annoyance, the spirit from his dream, with twelve other spirits, hovered before him, whirling in the air. The shadowy spirit, wearing a bow tie, paused to speak.

"I was a tax collector in life, the Mean Miser. How can you help me, or any of us to pass over? Can you pay my debts? Or help us home, to the other side? We need to rest, and we cannot rest here. Can you take us to the special place of passage, through the doorway? Christmas is coming, and I do not want to be here for another year."

Birrick felt annoyed and rubbed his eyes, then his medal, wondering what to say. "When I go over, perhaps I could take you with me, but first you must trust me and let me sleep."

"How can we trust you? How can we know or be certain? I need you to pay my debts. How can I take you seriously?" asked the tax collector.

"Have you no faith in elf nature?" replied Birrick.

"No, we have no faith in anything, which is why we are here now." A small phantom with a medical bag looked at Birrick quizzically. "I used to believe in medicine, but then I poisoned myself. I have no faith now. We need you to give us faith."

"Well, come with me, on my way to Malloway House. When I go over, at the end of my quest, you may be able to pass with me. Perhaps I can find a way to pay for the debts owed, and the deeds that have been done."

"When are you going through the eternal door?" asked the miserly tax man.

"Tomorrow night, it is the winter solstice soon. Come with me in the morning time when the sun rises."

"But we hide from the sun," remarked another, a thin female ghost, with a tiara on top of her head.

"Then hide in this purse, with the stones," and Birrick held open the pouch. The spirits looked interested, whispered to each other. Then slowly, one by one, all thirteen vanished into the pouch. Once the shadows disappeared, Birrick turned over to doze and dream a little longer, despite the cold. He looked forward in the night, to the morning which he knew would come.

Chapter Eleven

In the morning, a robin landed on Birrick's nose and started to sing. Birrick awoke, in annoyance, feeling slightly damp with the morning frost. Checking that he had his pouch; stones, medal, and feeling bright, he left the graveyard for the bus stop, where he waited for an early morning ride.

Along came a gypsy, driving a horse with a cart. As the gypsy rider rode past, he doffed his cap at Birrick, and shouted, "Greetings Marra!" passing by at a gentle pace. A black car, with an impatient driver, came up behind the cart, trying to overtake. As he did so, he tooted his horn. The horse reared, and the gypsy stood up to rein him in. Then the car passed, and there was no further incident. Ten minutes later, a large double-decker bus drew up at the stop. Birrick got out his elves' bus pass, clambering aboard.

"One to Malloway," said Birrick, showing his pass.

"Fine," replied the driver, an older man with love and hate tattooed on his knuckles, a red handkerchief in the driver's uniform pocket. Birrick took a seat at the back of the bus. Then, slowly, as he relaxed, the spirits came one by one out of the pouch, taking a seat for each one of them.

"Hey!" said Birrick. "Now what?"

"We haven't seen much apart from that graveyard for a long time," replied the Mean Miser.

Birrick wondered if the driver could see them, but the man didn't say anything. The small medical ghost floated around with his bag, inspecting the other passengers.

"Tut-tut," said the medical ghost, some of these people seem to be near death. "Shall I take your pulse?" he asked an old woman with a hearing aid. She heard nothing, and so the doctor sat next to Birrick, looking at him through a monocle.

"You don't look as if you're in good enough health. Can I check your throat?" he asked Birrick. "Have you been eating a healthy diet?" Suddenly it struck Birrick that he hadn't eaten in a long time. Even the singing hinnies, flapjacks, soup which he scoffed so eagerly were merely a food fantasy. The medical ghost tapped on Birrick's knees to check the reflexes, looked into his eyes, and peered into his mouth.

"Enough," said the ghost. "I see a spot! Out damned spot, out!"

"A spot, where?" asked Birrick.

"In your throat. I think it's very dangerous, even contagious, can I operate?"

Birrick involuntarily put his hand to his neck, looking the doctor in the eye of his monocle.

"I have a surgical implement; I think you are not long for this world! Let me try."

"Well," said Birrick. "Perhaps when we are er at Malloway House, now I just have to go upstairs to look at the view. Excuse me." Birrick stood up, clutching to the handrail on the stairs as he climbed up to the top of the moving bus.

Once at the top, Birrick could see open fields, small villages, isolated farms. There were old-fashioned cottages, odd ice-cream shops, and taverns by the roadside. An old female ghost, wearing her tiara, floated up the stairs.

"Are you looking forward to Christmas?" she asked, settling in front of Birrick. Then she started to sing an old song, which Birrick recognized.

"Weel may the keel row, the keel row, the keel row, weel may the keel row that my laddies in. As I went through Sandgate, through Sandgate, through Sandgate, as I went through Sandgate, I heard a lassie sing."

Birrick knew the song because Sally often sang it to him in the garden. Birrick felt suddenly sad, and wondered whether Sally had missed him, or would his mother have missed him in the Other World? The eternal door, and the potential passage through, would that be safe? Though he longed to be back there, to sit with the other elves and sprites under the sun, admire the angels, annoy the muses, would it be the same? Would he still be able to play on his golden flute in the place of angels?

Putting his hand inside his pouch, Birrick felt for the three stones, smooth, round, precious. Touching the medal at his neck, he wished to be back at Malloway House, soon.

A punk with a pink flat top hairstyle got on the bus. The young man sat on the top deck, at the front, reading 'The Times' quite openly. Birrick realized that Malloway Town was the next stop, and descended the stairs, followed by the ghost in her tiara.

Clutching the holding pole at the bus door, the thirteen ghosts hovered around him, then disappeared into his pouch. As Birrick waited, the bus stop loomed ahead. With a jerk, the bus halted to allow Birrick to dismount. Walking on, a sign was on the pavement with an arrow, it read, 'Psychic Tea

Shop, Weird Sisters This Way'. The arrow pointed down an alley and feeling hungry, Birrick followed it, into a small courtyard where a life-sized model of a waiter stood outside an open door. The fat waiter statue held in its hands a tea tray, bearing a bowl, on which were painted the words, 'Leave your tea leaves here'.

The café had dark curtains at the window, and Birrick had a strange feeling of chill as he entered through the small wooden doorway. Inside there were many black and purple velvet drapes, these were decorated with sequined stars, and there were various strangely shaped mirrors on the walls. Each dining table held a burning candle, there was a strong smell of patchouli, and a large glass cabinet displaying gothic jewellery, necklaces, rings, earrings. A large black teapot with a cat effigy stood on the counter next to many weirdly shaped cakes. Birrick stepped a little closer, there were cakes in the shape of skulls, bats, cats, and snakes, with green coloured icing. Looking up, he noticed a puppet in the form of a witch hanging above the till.

Birrick sat at a large oval table, and the thirteen ghosts came out to sit with him. There was an open newspaper, the 'Daily Augur', on the front page of which Birrick could see a picture of the Citadel. The Citadel is the place of power and government in the Present Lands. Underneath the picture of the turreted Citadel, Birrick read the lines, "Government in Crisis, in the Citadel the Conference of Elves are in revolt, the Tower of Keys and the Tower of Laws cannot agree on policy, Lamguin the Blade is in hiding, our leader has not been seen for a month. The future of many fortune tellers and prediction rights are insecure, a generation of soothsayers may become unemployable. A dark cloud of bats has settled on the Citadel, while the mess of legislation and the lack of controlled magic could bring the dark times on us again." Beneath this was a picture of Lamguin's office, showing an empty desk. A further caption read, "Turn to page five for more."

A strange woman all in silver came to wait on Birrick. "What can I get you?" she asked.

Birrick rubbed the back of his neck, "One skull cake, and a mug of hot black magic chocolate with marshmallows please."

"Would you like cream on top?"

"Yes," replied Birrick, feeling a little scared of the woman all in red at the next table. She smiled at him. Birrick felt his skin creep, and he picked up the newspaper. About ten seconds later, or as quickly as you could say 'hey presto', the hot chocolate arrived, placed on the table by the silver waitress. Draining his cup, the marshmallows formed the shape of a strange-looking monster. The cake appeared, and Birrick reached out his hand, but as if by a sixth sense, the cake moved away from him, and the mug drifted off the table. The red woman laughed, a cackle, the silver woman joined her, and another woman dressed in black appeared from behind a drape. Birrick looked hard, there they were; Rowan, Yew, and Hazel. Suddenly Yew raised her hand, showing long dark fingernails like talons. Pointing a finger at Birrick, she started to recant her witchery spell.

"Double trouble, chocolate bubble, magic come and make him crumble, put this elf under my spell. Witchcraft help me to do well."

Immediately another Birrick appeared before his eyes, he recoiled as the witches laughed. He tried to run but found his feet were like lead. Hazel came up to him, holding a collar with chain, which she started to swing, menacing Birrick with her evil grin. Birrick was petrified, feeling too heavy to move. Then, as if by a reflex memory, he put his hand to his neck, touching the medal there. Rubbing it, hope flooded through his feet and up to his body, and he felt strong. Drawing a circle in the air, he cast this around himself, so that the circle glowed around him. Hazel, Yew, and Rowan stood still, and time stood still. The other Birrick crumbled into a heap of sand on the floor. The witches drew together, standing in a trio back-to-back. Birrick lifted a circular mirror from the wall, holding it up aloft. Shouting out "intra minimus reflectus", he held the mirror to catch the reflections of the weird sisters. Screaming, and swirling in their gowns, they whirled in a vortex, disappearing into the mirror. Birrick calmly placed the mirror back on the wall and smiled at the faces of the witches who were trapped in the mirror, looking out.

The ghosts applauded him, and disappeared back into the pouch, but not before the Miser could say, "And remember my debts, remember the doorway, tonight, it must be tonight, remember that."

Leaving with the newspaper under his arm, the witches trapped in their world of glass, Birrick turned down the high street. He intended to cut through the woods, taking a shorter route to Malloway House. Birrick shrugged to himself, patting his purse pouch, and wondering what Sally would say when he showed up with stones, ghosts, and a peculiar silver key.

Entering the Elder Woods, Birrick noticed a piece of white cloth flapping in the wind. It was tied to a branch of an Elder tree. Walking onwards there were other pieces, also ribbons, some red, some brown, some white, tied to different trees.

Going up close and examining one piece of cloth, there was writing on it. The message read, 'Here is the last chance, to come and join our dance'. A man in a long brown robe came up to Birrick. "Have you seen the others?" he asked.

"The others?" Birrick replied, surprised.

"The other druids," the man continued. "We are here to pass the shortest day, the longest night, to remember the year's dying light. The meeting is in the woods."

Suddenly a deer ran past them, going south, and the druid said, "That must be the way." Then they walked in the direction that the animal ran.

High above the tallest trees, Birrick could see the old gibbet where they used to hang people for crimes. He thought he could see a body, swinging from it. He gulped. Feeling a sense of urgency, he quickened his pace through the trees. Taking out the newspaper, 'Daily Augur' to read as he walked, Birrick turned to page five. The story read...

"Lamguin had received threats of a hideous nature. Not only the usual spell grabbing, but money taking threats, also a threat of a different sort, of a more serious type. Scientists, academics are trying to control the Citadel. A threat had been made on his life, so he disappeared to protect his own safety.. Now, with any further damage to the Citadel, to the seat of power, a threat which comes from the Dark Lands of the Underworld, and those who inhabit such places, the White Beast may try to return. We have been informed by our mole, that this threat is considered serious enough. The Two Towers, the Tower of Laws, and the Tower of Keys are seeking to appoint a deputy to manage a coalition administration in Lamguin's absence. No suitable candidate has yet been found. Who knows what will come to pass should the White Beast return?" Birrick wrinkled his brow, putting his newspaper inside his jacket pocket.

Chapter Twelve

Walking further, Birrick could see a group of men, dressed in brown, sitting under a large oak tree. A deer stood among the group. Birrick approached them thoughtfully, trying to think of a greeting. They were druids. The deer came up to him, nuzzling its wet velvety nose in his hand. Then the deer gambolled off on its long legs, leaving Birrick to face the group alone.

One of the men shouted to Birrick, "Would you like to join us? You could be our sacrifice? So far all we have is a scarecrow."

Birrick looked for the straw man, then noticed the body swinging from the gibbet, it was made of straw and rags. The crowd laughed, and Birrick realized that they were drinking from bottles or flasks.

"We could do with an elfin John Barleycorn," said a bald druid out loud. "Surely you would like to join the dance?"

Birrick looked for a further moment, scared, heart still, then he ran. As he ran he dodged trees and bushes. Bottles were thrown after him, and in a fleeting thought, Birrick wondered whether the druids were drunk. Birrick kept running in what he thought was the right direction. He knew the stories of the man sacrificed to the gods and left in the fields. The earthen gods, the old way. Abruptly, Birrick came to a road. A badger streaked across, and Birrick followed, tripping on a tree root. He fell, and as he fell he cursed his luck, falling into a rivulet which ran along a ditch.

Wet and worried, Birrick tried to catch his breath, his pulse beating at three times the normal elfin rate. Looking into the stream, at his reflection, he saw another face beside his own. A man's face, a face marked with tattoos, reading 'night' on one cheekbone, and 'day' on the other. The man had no hair, but his bald head was covered in tattoos as well as his face. Starting to talk, the face said, "I am the Dark Dreamer, from the Dark Lands. You elf have entered my dreams, trod on my conscience, and now you are in my stream. You, elf, have a wish for secrets. Come to me, I will give you secrets." A wrinkled hand stretched out, up out of the stream, and dragged Birrick under. He, struggling, coughing, had no power over the Dreamer. The Dreamer's world of weeds, wishes, dreams, or nightmares was pulling at Birrick, drawing him down.

Closing his eyes tightly, and counting to ten, Birrick found on opening his eyes, that he was in a darkened room, with a red light glowing in one corner. The Dreamer, wrapped in a red wool cloak, sat on an old rocking chair. For a few seconds, there was quiet, then the Dreamer spoke aloud in a raspingly scary voice, like a person with a sore throat.

"Birrick, elf, you are an adventurer. You have travelled a long way, looking for secrets. Now I am telling you my secrets. You can have power, in my darkest dreams, in my world of no hope, you can bring despair. You can follow me and be mine."

Birrick stared, then said, "Er…otherwise?"

"Look into the red light, Birrick. What can you see?"

Looking, Birrick saw a woman, burning in a car crash. Biting his lip, he realized the woman was Sally.

"Give me the stones," said the Dreamer, "and I will give you powers."

"And if I say no?"

"Then people will die, and you will be unable to break my spell. You will be a prisoner, in my conscience, forever. I can create a new dream for you, it is a kind of nightmare, if you do not give me the stones, you will remain in this state, you will never be free of this dream. Here I have the Dark Child, Ciarra, she is coming to haunt you." The small form of Ciarra stepped out from the light, and her eyes gleamed with hate, as she showed teeth like fangs.

Birrick knew that the Dreamer only wanted one answer, but he in his elfin mind thought that there could be another way. Ciarra stretched out her hand, and as her fingers seemed to grow longer, her nails reached out to scratch him.

"Ow!" he cried, as she drew blood. Birrick rubbed his hand, his mind racing. Then he knew.

"I don't believe you," he shouted. "You are only in my dreams. 'Dies de muertes, noches de mea voles, spiritus venga'." The thirteen spirits left the pouch, circling the Dreamer and his child, until the pair cowed in the corner, in front of the red light. Picking up the light, the Dreamer threw it at Birrick. It missed and smashed on the floor in many pieces. All was darkness, Birrick closed his eyes, and counted to thirteen.

Feeling a chill, Birrick gasped and found himself in the open air, standing by the stream. The spirits, raising from the waters, danced in the dappled shade of the trees.

"That was fortunate," said the spectral doctor, the Dreamer was nowhere to be seen. Birrick held up his key, and the ghosts about him sang sweetly, a rhyme that he had known as a child elf. "Here for a day, night passes away, in our dreams we dance today." The spirits circled him once more, then vanished back into the pouch, one at a time.

Birrick threw a stone into the stream, hoping to hit the Dreamer on the nose. All he could see were the pebbles at the bottom, and a few small fish amid floating leaves. Drawing a circle around himself with the key, he pulled a sprig of ivy that cascaded down from an old tree. Putting the ivy in his buttonhole, to strengthen his defences he started singing 'The Holly and the Ivy'. Mounting the bank of the ditch, the key drew him on, down the road. A roe deer ran in front of him, and he wondered if this was the same deer he saw in the Elder Woods. Feeling that all might be well, he looked at the sky for some indication of what would come.

It was still winter in the Present Lands, a cold north wind caused Birrick to pull his collar up, the sky was blue and grey, yet the sun still shone.

Looking to the left, then to the right, Birrick could see a group of houses beside a small church. After a while, he recognized the weathervane, a brass cockerel on the church steeple. Malloway House was, he knew, close by. Reaching an old wooden gate, which opened onto a long garden, Birrick paused, then went through. There was the fishpond, the old oak tree with its treehouse, and Sally, in the garden, planting bulbs. Birrick approached the pond, and sat on the wall, next to the shed where he used to sleep. He waited quietly without saying a word, wondering if Sally would notice him. Looking at his reflection in the fishpond, he could see that his aura glowed silver as well as gold. Had he, after all, done enough?

Sally stood up to fetch some more bulbs, as she straightened herself, she saw Birrick, poised to tell his tale. Smiling, she went up to him.

"Well?" she asked.

"Ahem?" replied Birrick.

"Have you brought me the necessary?" she enquired. "The proof of the Other World, the stone of second sight, a tale to tell?"

Birrick looked at Sally, "It's cold." he said. "Let's go inside. I need to warm up before recanting any adventures."

"OK, let's go in, and you can tell me all about it."

"How long have I been gone?" he asked.

"About a week, give or take a day or two. I knew you would be back. Here." She opened the blue front door, and they passed inside.

Sitting in the kitchen among sprigs of holly and mistletoe, Birrick started to tell what he knew.

"You want proof of the Other World? Here." He opened his pouch, tipping out the three blue stones onto the kitchen table, and then he murmured, "exitus spiritus, spiritus videmus." The thirteen ghosts slowly left the pouch, materializing in the kitchen, floating above the table, then, with a look from Birrick. They seated themselves on the trestles beside the table.

The ghostly doctor spoke first, "We have come here to pass over, it is the solstice, the time of Yule. We need to make our way, with your help, through the Eternal Doorway."

The taxman cleared his throat, "I need to find a way to pay my debts to enter the place of rest. Perhaps you can pay them for me?"

The old ghost, wearing her tiara chimed in, "What do you think of the stones? They are quite beautiful, aren't they?"

Sally looked at the stones, then at the spirits, speechless for a few seconds as she swallowed hard.

"We wove a spell," continued Birrick. "The Guardian, the Seer, and me. Take them and you will be blessed with second sight, but if you take them you must help us all, otherwise, I cannot help but fear the consequences."

Sally shivered, and a clock chimed twelve, it was midday. "Very well, you can go. I will find a way to help you all, and you can go to the Other World on the other side of the rainbow. Just make sure to let me know when you have got there, I want proof, not just humbug."

"Hoorah!" shouted the thirteen spirits.

"But," said Birrick, "You need to help us to open the Eternal Doorway."

"And how can I do that?" asked Sally, looking at Birrick.

"Only at the midnight hour, the doorway opens, and you must light a candle, say a prayer, a wish, a spell, then we will pass through. Tonight, say you will do this tonight. It is the solstice, it makes passing easier, a time to settle old scores or pay favours. But, we can only go with your goodwill, bad will holds a spirit back." The doctor spoke, and then…

"Say aye," said Birrick.

Sally looked at the spirits, she looked at Birrick, and said, "Aye. Alright, aye to you. There will be a party tonight, here, with a séance. All of you are invited."

"Excellent!" said Birrick. "Do you have a Yule log and a Yule wreath?"

"Yes," Sally answered. "I've been saving them for you."

The ghosts cheered. "We need a good rest," said the doctor. "I haven't slept in one hundred years."

"Then sleep in the attic. There are cushions and blankets there. I have to prepare for the party. It's a fancy-dress séance. You must turn up and scare people for me. My friends would like to see a real ghost! Birrick will take you to the attic, I still have a lot of cooking to do."

Chapter Thirteen

The old Victorian house had long corridors and a winding stair banister. Birrick leapt onto the rail, and slid upwards, shouting, "Wheeeee, it's Christmas! Haunting tonight!" Several old pictures hung on the walls, decorated with tinsel. Passing the picture of Oscar Wilde, he turned to look. Oscar winked, and Birrick winked back. The ghosts followed him, floating, muttering, singing, rattling their jewellery, or their chains. The tax collector, who carried a particularly long chain, hung it on the hat stand, along with his hat. In the attic, a large lofty room with a skylight window, the ghosts lay down to rest, as did Birrick. They would need their ghouling skills for the party.

Sally took the three moonstones and plodded up the stairs to the first floor. On the landing was an old-fashioned ottoman chair, carved in wood. She lifted the seat lid and took out some linen sheets. Underneath was a box of tarot cards, some old books, an old bell, and a small box with a mother of pearl inlay. Taking out the box, she put the moonstones inside, along with a picture of her long-dead husband, and a broach in gold which he had given her. The broach, a golden sprig held the message, 'Forget me not'. Taking the broach out, she put everything else back inside the ottoman and returned to the kitchen to bake for the party. The old stairs creaked as she descended, but then, so did she.

After a while, the ghosts revived and started practicing their haunting rituals. Birrick however, remained asleep on a cushion, with Teabag, Sally's cat curled up beside him. He was dreaming, and in his dream, he was back by the stream. Many fish swam by, mostly brown, some silver. One particularly blackfish jumped out of the water and landed beside Birrick on the grassy bank. Birrick picked up the fish and held onto it as it wriggled. The fish started to change colour, first turning orange, then white, then gold. The fish opened and shut its mouth helplessly, so that Birrick, feeling sorry, gently lowered it into the stream. The fish turned to look at him, then swam off to follow its friends further down in the water. It was warm in the attic, and as Birrick slept old memories came to him of carolling, chasing angels, partying. Then a dark shadow passed over into the dreamworld which Birrick knew, it was a bald man with tattoos, the Dreamer.

The Dreamer glared, and at first, Birrick could only see his face and bald pate. The large brown eyes with no white stared with a hypnotic pull.

"Birrick, Birrick," said the Dreamer quietly. "Come to me. There is still time for you, I will give you wonderful powers, secrets, dreams. I will help you to realise yourself, you can have everything Birrick, but you must give up the Other World, give up your innocence, your hardships, your soul-life, your very inner essence. Come to me Birrick, I will show you a whole new world, a whole new reality is waiting for you. I can give you the power of the inner eye, of serendipity, of wishes, come true. I can give you everything, everything you wish for, this is your chance now." The Dreamer held out a hand to Birrick. Birrick turned on his side in his sleep, to turn away. Suddenly Teabag's fur went up Birrick's nose, so that he sneezed, coughed, and awoke.

As Birrick returned to wakefulness, he realized that the Dreamer was no longer in control. But Birrick also knew that the dark tattooed figure did have some power through dreams. Birrick hoped that in passing to the Other World he would leave this behind. Teabag meowed so that Birrick started to stroke the cat. The pretty green eyes, whiskers, fur, spots on the nose, and various cat features made Teabag attractive even to Birrick. He thought of Mr Cheese, the witches' pet, the strange creatures which they kept. Teabag seemed quite normal in comparison, and Sally suddenly seemed a decent friend. Birrick knew the problems of humans, even Sally's problems. The awful boyfriends, false people, takers. Some come to give, and those who come to take. Dreams are powerful things, but are they always real? Teabag could not be false, nor could Sally. Birrick suddenly felt a craving for a cup of tea.

Leaving the ghosts and venturing down the stairs, along the corridor into the kitchen, Birrick found Sally cutting the pastry into stars. Clearing his throat, he said, "Ahem."

"Yes?" Sally replied, "What's the problem?"

"Er…could you make me a pot of tea, please? I would love a cup of char."

Sally turned to look at Birrick, taking him seriously, "What kind of tea would you like? Lapsang Souchong, Earl Grey, Darjeeling?"

"Do you have any English Breakfast Tea? I feel a strong thirst for things that are English today."

"Certainly, and soon you will be off tonight, so in that case, here is your tea." She handed him a china mug, steaming, with the teabag still in it. Birrick poured in some milk from a jug on the table and fished out the bag. Sipping it carefully, he sat watching Sally baking.

"Are you going to tell me about your adventures Birrick?" she asked.

Birrick looked into the tea. "Well, it's complicated. There were several quite nasty scrapes, even a few shocks. Perhaps I will tell you more later. There were strange cats with human faces, at one point I had to fight off a terrible worm. For what seemed like many days I travelled underground, there is a whole network of interlinking mine tunnels, north of the Wall, where wizards, bats, strange creatures live. A Guardian came to help me many times, a woman who only had one eye."

"Do you still want to go back to the Other World, Birrick? Is it so wonderful there?" Sally asked.

"Well yes. You see, there it is always summer, the gardens are always beautiful, fountains spray water with many lights. We have singing, parties, people recover from ill health, and there is happiness there, in a simple life. You can't say that they care for this. The Present Lands don't worry you at times. No cars to crash, no bills to pay, no arguments too bad, or if they do catch you arguing you get kicked out of course. Yes, that's happened, smoking isn't allowed either. Also, I must tell you, Sally, to drive more carefully, and beware a hook."

"A hook?"

"Yes, I think someone might try fishing in your pond. Those fish look tasty and expensive."

"Oh well, recently, I caught my favourite dress on a coat hanger hook. I had to sew up the tare. Though that doesn't seem as serious as the fishing."

"Right, and stay out of the woods, stay away from the stream."

"Why?"

"There are druids, and dark shadows, I don't like the look of them."

"Oh, they're harmless, Birrick. Druids respect nature and shadows hurt no one."

"That's what you think!" said Birrick, swallowing the last of his tea.

"You will be warning me about vampires and werewolves next, Birrick."

"They might have been there too, but the wolf was a friend, Crimthain. Perhaps he might have eaten a child or two, but friendly. One other thing…" Birrick's voice trailed off.

"Yes?"

"Have you read the 'Daily Augur'?"

"No, I haven't."

"Hmm, here is a copy, I kept it for you. There is a very nasty story inside."

"Oh?"

"Yes, about Lamguin and the Citadel. The government is in trouble again."

Birrick took the copy out of his jacket and passed it to Sally.

"So, what happened to the wolf?" she enquired.

"He died; he couldn't live forever. Now, before I go and give your fish the last farewell, for friendship's sake, why don't you tell me the story of the curse?"

"Er, the curse?" Sally asked.

"Yes, the curse of Malloway House. Tell me, you never told me all the time that I gazed on your goldfish, tell me now."

"Well, Birrick, the curse, which is also the curse of our present time, is that we want our reward now, not in the Other World. The last owner of this house, before me, tried to have it all, and killed his wife, burying her body in the woods, to have other wives. The first wife haunted him and cursed him so that whoever lives here cannot be happy for long. The man sold me the house for a song, to escape the curse."

"Then why do you live here?"

"I gave up trying to be happy years ago. I just want to know secrets and do the garden. The dead will help me. I do not care much for the living. My curse is in a sense to know and want to know more. A further problem is that people always want more, and this is a problem for our land, the Present Land, as we struggle for what we want. It is a quandary which we all face, in our time."

"Can't you want less?" asked Birrick.

"Only with difficulty, that is the truth."

"Why is that?"

"We believe in greed, and that's why. Most people think that bigger is better, and getting better than giving." Sally sighed and turned to roll out some more dough.

Putting down the now empty tea mug, Birrick decided to venture off into the cold December air, for the last look at the garden, the pond, even the gnome, and Sally's fish, swimming like golden ghosts, haunting the green pond waters. Whilst staring into the pond, a feeling of intense cold crept over Birrick. As he watched the fish in the waters, the image of the

Dark Dreamer started to form, so that Birrick could make out the tattooed face in the pond. As Birrick stared, he felt drawn to the water, but he also felt afraid. The Dreamer did not say anything, he looked, he stared with large dark eyes, emanating a hypnotic pull. The menacing glare, those tattoos were off-putting, yet Birrick could not help but feel a sense of attraction to something darker, deeper than himself. "Turn away," whispered the voice of Mr Unreal. "Turn away, Birrick. You must, or you risk losing your willpower and strength. Turn, now, turn away." Birrick heard a bird call, and, easing his gaze away from the pond to the garden, the wildlife around him, he felt relief. A small robin was sitting on the bird table, as its mate sat pecking the birdfeeder for food. Birrick glanced again at the pond. The Dreamer had gone, in his place were only fish. Birrick shrugged and continued to inspect the garden in the cold winter light.

Back inside, Sally read the newspaper which Birrick had left her. Looking at the pictures and reading the news about Lamguin, she felt a sense of sadness. There was a further article about the White Beast, who had been banned twenty-five years ago, in the last century. What would happen to the Present Lands if he returned to a position of power. Lamguin in hiding, what now? The forces could always build-up, particularly at this special time of year. Should the Citadel lose control, anything, yes anything might happen, become possible or impossible, flying fish, broken rainbows, pigs that talked. This in itself could raise problems for decent folk who wanted to live peaceably, with the odd spell, visitation, or experiment not too difficult to manage or live with, under a reasonable government. Putting the newspaper to one side with a pile of history magazines, she checked the sweet mince pies that were in the oven, taking them out to make way for the next batch of sweet treats. She heard a knock at the back door. Going to answer, it was Birrick. She welcomed him inside.

Chapter Fourteen

Come eleven p.m., it was time for the celebrations to begin. Sally had dressed, complete with a blonde bob-shaped wig and nineteen twenties dress. The inner room, where the séance would be held, was clean, tidy, and a large mahogany oval table dominated the centre of the room, a piano in the recess. Aside from Sally, Birrick, and the ghosts, there would be six guests. These guests numbered among them; Dr Diaz, Mrs Bright, Miss Twilight, Mr Morningstar, Mr Richlady, and Miss Hood. A strange crew, knocking on the white front door of Malloway House at about eleven fifteen, just as Sally was wondering whether anyone would arrive at all.

"Good evening," said Mr Morningstar, resplendent in a black top hat, evening coat, and cane.

"How are you?" asked Miss Hood, standing on the doorstep in her red outfit with matching red hooded cape.

"It's time," said Miss Twilight, her grey eyeshadow sparkling along with her silver glittered hair in the light from a lamp post. Her grey gown shimmered with sequins under a grey faux fur wrap.

"Can we come in?" queried Mr Richlady, twiddling his curled moustache like the curls on his forehead. Then he put his thumbs in his striped waistcoat, revealing a watch chain.

"I believe the spirits will be with us tonight," said Mrs Bright, in her green crimplene frock, high heels, and gay green fascinator. Knocking impatiently on the door she shouted through the letterbox, "Let us in, let us in! I'm sure you have some surprises for us."

"It's cold as death out here," remarked Dr Diaz, looking down at Sally as she opened the door. He stood at seven feet high. "The night air is chilly, we are waiting, present and correct."

Sally smiled, "Come in then, all of you enter now, we will have spirit friends with us tonight. Just leave your coats in the cloakroom. The food is ready, the spirits are waiting for us."

"And we will be in good spirits ourselves," said Mr Richlady as he took off his scarf, "We have been looking forward to a night of entertainment. I could do with a large whisky now, and a good spooky scare at the spooky meeting, I had a bad enough day in court today. Who said that ley magistrates get it easy?"

"In court, huh?"

"Yes, I have responsibilities."

"In here," said Sally, ushering her guests into the inner room. Immediately, the medical ghost sat at the piano, and started to play Beethoven's 'Moonlight Sonata'.

"Who are you?" asked Mr Richlady.

"I am the ghost of science past, I have come to bring proof to those who do not believe," echoed the spirit doctor, levitating over the dining table and floating around the room.

"Dear me," said Mrs Bright, "and what a lovely spread." The food was laid out on the oval table, so the guests went to serve themselves. A hand appeared from nowhere and lifted up Dr Diaz's wig. The wig whizzed around in the air, landing on an unlit candelabra. Mr Richlady started laughing, and Dr Diaz was blushing. Suddenly a tall, cobwebbed woman in an old-fashioned style tiara and dress sat on the black marble mantelpiece. From where she perched, she looked down on her audience.

"I am the ghost of disappointed love. Call me Dolores," she said, cobwebs floating around her. "I have come to warn you of the problems you are storing for yourselves, as the ghosts of the twentieth century see the problems of the twenty-first. You are piling up many ill-wishes, which can rebound on you. We have not been able to pass because of ill-feeling. Cause too much ill-will and you will have more difficulties yourselves. You must listen tonight." Dolores laughed, a haunting laugh, and vanished.

Mrs Twilight sparkled suddenly in the firelight, "Let's finish eating, then have our séance. Surely the spirits can wait for us."

Birrick, hiding beneath the table, heard her, and muttered, "If you don't eat up soon then I'll be scaring you as well."

"What was that?" asked Miss Hood.

"Oh nothing," said Sally, who was serving drinks. "Here have a little wine." Pouring Miss Hood a glass of rose, Sally also sat at the table, kicking Birrick on the nose as she crossed her legs.

"What's your new year's resolution?" asked Dr Diaz of the group at large.

"Oh, to lose some weight and paint a decent picture for a change," said Sally. "I recently painted a terrible self-portrait, but first I need to improve my looks before I try again."

"And you?" Dr Diaz turned his focus onto Mrs Bright.

"To have my newest cat neutered, she had another litter last week. Would anyone like a kitten?"

"Oh, that reminds me," said Miss Morningstar. "I need to regularly put some food out for the birds."

"Yes yes, the birds could suffer. And what about you, Miss Hood, what's your resolution?"

"Oh, to tame a wolf."

"Interesting, a wild wolf?"

"No, a lone wolf. They're more dangerous. But what about Mr Richlady, what is his new year wish?"

"To change my name and get a decent haircut. Now then doctor, your turn."

"To raise the dead."

The room lit up suddenly as the electric lighting started to flash and the candelabra pendant light swung wildly. The curtains billowed, a chill draught passed through the room, a tinkling of bells could be heard.

"What's that?" asked Mr Richlady. Sally stood up to light the white waxen candles on the black mantelpiece.

"Now friends, shall we start? Shall we turn our attention to the spirit world?"

"But of course," said Mrs Bright, eagerly. Sally cleared the food to one side, on the sideboard. From the drawer, she produced the cards for Ouija, which she lay around the table. A downturned glass was placed in the centre.

"Let us begin," said Sally. The group sat solemnly with their eyes closed, hands on the cold hard wooden surface.

"We seek to communicate with the spirits tonight," intoned Dr Diaz. "Spirits, is there anything you have to say to us, any warning or secret or sign to give?"

108

With that, every member of the group put their right index finger on the upturned glass. Slowly, the glass started to move. Birrick knocked twice on the underside of the table, and Sally kicked him again. The glass spelled out, "S.O.S., I am lost, help me."

"Who are you?" asked Dr Diaz.

"I was a soldier from County Mayo. I died in the Great War," spelled the glass. One of the spirits, in his army uniform, circled the table.

"Are there others?" asked Dr Diaz

"Yes," spelled the glass, and all thirteen spirits manifested in the inner room as shadows in the candlelight, dancing, whirling, moaning, whispering, "Save our souls, save our souls. Before midnight tonight, give us our passing rights." The wall clock chimed half eleven, and as the ghosts danced, Dr Diaz sat with his mouth open. Birrick appeared from under the table and cleared his throat.

"Help us to go through the eternal doorway, at this time of Yule, help us tonight."

"Here is the bell," he said and handed Sally the old brass bell from the mantelpiece.

Ringing the bell, Sally said in a loud voice, "Once for luck, twice for death, thrice to take an extra breath. We open the doorway here tonight, to help you pass over, without any fight. Take your leave, go into the light. Pass through, pass through, pass through on this, the longest night."

The candle flames extinguished, the room darkened, and the group sat there waiting in expectation as the spirits passed through the fireside mirror into a world of rest.

"Well, that's torn it," said Birrick, standing beside the fire, "I'm still here!" Scratching his head, he looked at the group, the only light coming from the fire.

"Birrick," said Sally, "to pay all accrued debts of yourself and the spirits, you must pass with a gift."

"Gift?" he asked.

"Here," she took a wreath from the doorway of holly and mistletoe, intertwined with the sprigs were several gold charms.

"Take it, with your elf magic you may need this. Tonight, you have free passage, but…"

"What but?" asked Birrick.

"But give me a sign, when you have got to the Other World give me a sign so that I will know the truth."

"Very well, if you wish it," said Birrick.

Again, Sally rang the bell, thirteen times, the sound reverberating around the room.

A golden-haired woman appeared in a white robe, the one green eye-opening in her forehead. The gathering of friends let out a gasp, amazed at the wonderful beauty of the strange woman. The room filled with the scent of roses.

"I am the Guardian," said the messenger, "and Birrick must come with me. We must go to the Citadel, there isn't much time left."

"But I want to go to the Other World," complained Birrick.

"In good time," replied the Guardian. "Come with me." She took the wreath Sally offered in one hand, and taking Birrick's elfin paw in the other, she started to sing. The group listened intently to the silver tones in her voice, "This ae nicht, this ae nicht, every nicht and all, and fire and fleet and candle licht. The light receives thy soul."

Her white robe swirled out, enveloping Birrick and herself. Suddenly the candles were aflame again, Birrick and the Guardian hovered momentarily. Sally sneezed, closing her eyes. When she opened them, where had the pair had gone?

Sally got up from the table, she could see something on the rug in front of the fire, picking it up, she realized it was a perfect red apple that the Guardian had left behind.

"Where did you meet that strange young man?" asked Mrs Bright.

"Oh, I found him living in my shed, in the garden. That's where he slept. Shall we sing? I can play a tune on the piano."

"Yes," said Dr Diaz. "We have seen enough spirits for tonight."

Suddenly, there was a loud banging. The group hushed and listened.

Sally went to the French window; she could see a dark figure outside.

"Let me in," shouted the Dreamer, "Let me in."

Closing the curtain, Sally returned to her friends.

"Who is it?" asked Mr Richlady.

"Only a stranger, no one I know. Leave him and he will go away."

Crowding around the piano, the group sang on, into the early hours, oblivious to all but the early morning music and the stars in the late-night sky.

Chapter Fifteen

In the Citadel, another late-night story was evolving. The Conference of Elves were in a heated meeting of arguments, and motions.

"And I declare," said Philo, "that we elves have put up with enough, for far too long. We need to assert ourselves, our position in government is an important one. The Two Towers cannot pass laws without our consent, yet they do not heed our warnings, our voice. Now the two upper chambers are in deadlock. They cannot agree. Lamguin is gone, the Tower of Laws and the Tower of Keys are useless without us. There have been riots on the streets of Carmion, even our place here isn't safe without good government. We cannot have magic, or violence breaking out all over the place. The Towers should come to an agreement with our help. We need to act quickly before worse comes to pass, and before the dark times descend once more."

A cheer went up from the elves. Birrick, sitting quietly at the back with the Guardian, opened his eyes wide, looking at the hall they were in. There was a high ceiling, with many wooden carvings. The walls, covered in wooden panelling, held a series of stone masks, gargoyles, and wall hangings.

"So, you see the problem Birrick," said the Guardian to him. "Now, as you are still in my care, you have to help me to sort this out."

Birrick gulped. "What can I do here?"

"Philo will befriend you if you approach him. You still have the key, so he will trust you. Together, you will mastermind the Citadel until the threat of the dark days and pandemonium has gone."

"But how am I going to do any good in this situation? Surely, I am just a junior elf."

"You have passed your quest Birrick, and that means you know enough. Once a person passes their test, they move upwards to other goals."

"Why?" Birrick asked.

"To be useful, to avoid being a drongo. Besides, if the government of the Present Lands goes berserk, that will cause an even worse situation. Then everyone will try to get to the Other World, and we are very particular over who we allow in! We can't all go there easily. The White Beast must not take control either. He is trying to and has friends. You are called Birrick; I, the Guardian, am commanding you."

Birrick sighed, realized he couldn't think of a good enough argument, so he turned to look the Guardian in her eye. The one beautiful green eye opened wide in her forehead. Birrick knew he was under her protection. Malloway House suddenly seemed a peaceful place. There he was, in the Citadel, surrounded by elves, drat; how could he get away now?

The cheering of the elves died down, Philo started shouting, "We must go now, to the highest office, so that the Towers give in to our demands. Come, we will advance the position of elves. Elves will no longer be drongos or do-it-alls. We will unite the Citadel! follow me!"

With that, the double doors of the conference suite flew open. Hats were thrown in the air; whooping, and shouting, the elves crowded through. The Guardian said to Birrick, "You will not fail. You will not be a drongo," and then vanished. Birrick reluctantly joined the crowd before him.

Pushing on up the wide sweeping staircase with its wooden balustrade, the elves made their way to the upper rooms of the Citadel. To the right of the wide landing was the hall of the Tower of Keys, with its many windows and rows of seats. To the left, the hall of the Tower of Laws. The two were similar, except the Tower of Keys was carpeted in red and the Tower of Laws carpeted in blue. The stone floor of the landing was made of uneven flags, bordered with potted shrubs, between which were many wooden doors. There were many portraits of past dignitaries on the walls. One tall door had a golden plaque with undecipherable lettering. Philo pushed open the door. Two men were sitting at a leather-covered desk. Both wore a grey wig to cover their natural hair. One wore what looked like a priest's clothes, the other jeans, boots, and a jerkin. Standing up as Philo entered with the other elves, the taller of the two men frowned fiercely.

Scowling he said, "You, elves! What brings you here?"

"Bede, Lugh, I have come to play my role in government at a time of need. We have come to assert the rights of elves, of the peoples of the Present Lands. As the pair of you seem to be having trouble, we have decided to join you by giving our opinion. If things go on the way they have been for much longer; the rioting, the food shortages, the uncontrolled magic, the Academics will get the upper hand. We have come to guide you."

Bede the priest and Lugh the Celt looked at Philo and laughed.

"But you are just an elf," said Bede.

Birrick, feeling annoyed spoke up, "Elves can have brains. We can weave spells or laws just as much as you. Do not look down on us just because we aren't six foot tall with a wig on!"

Philo pointed to a small hammer on the table; "Give me the gavel. I, Philo, am a friend to many. We have come to prevent further disorder, to prevent the regrouping of the Conference of Academics, with the White Beast as their leader. Give me the gavel. In the absence of Lamguin, we will rule together. I have led the conference for many years, I will help you because I am an elf."

So, saying, Philo, a slightly taller elf, grabbed the hammer, striking the table with it three times.

Suddenly Bede and Lugh sat down. Taking off their wigs, they looked at each other.

"What shall we do?" asked Lugh.

Bede answered, "Give in. Now is not a time to argue. We need help now."

Bede smiled, Birrick noticed that the windows seemed unnaturally dark, then he realized that they were covered with squeaking bats.

"You need a rule of right-mindedness," said Philo.

"Yes, and I suppose we can't decide on much without Lamguin. You have taken the gavel. There is one thing left to give." Bede drew a long chain up from around his waist. On it was a set of golden keys. Unhitching a very ornate gold key,

Bede lifted it aloft. "Here," he said. "The balance of powers lies with you Philo, as a triumvirate, we may succeed."

Lugh shrugged his shoulders. Philo took the key and put it on his key ring, which went through a jacket buttonhole.

The elves cried out in delight, "We rule together! We rule tonight! We rule with all our elvish might! The power of three will set things to rights."

"Very well," said Lugh, "as a representative of the Lords, I accept you."

"And I, from the cloth, accept you, but remember," said Bede, "it is with our consent. Elves do not normally hold such power; we are making an exception. Lamguin was a war Lord, of real skill. He had proven himself many times. You also, Philo, will have to prove your power."

"I will be of service to you, Philo," said Birrick, from his place inside the doorway. "I swear my allegiance to you, and the lives in the Citadel."

"Who are you?" queried Bede, warily.

"My name is Birrick. I am a tried and tested elf, on a long journey of fidelity. A friend sent me to you. Here is my key." He held aloft the gleaming silver antique key. Philo turned to look at it, touching the strange key with its old runic script in his hands. Taking Birrick by the shoulders, Philo said, "Now I believe you; you will come with me." Then shouting, "Fellow elves, let's go to the Coven Bar to celebrate. A new era is dawning in our history. Friends, we will lead the Citadel to safety yet! I will stand you all a mug of hot chocolate."

Pushing with Birrick through the crowd, they made their way to the basement Coven Bar. Philo ordered his drinks from a witch, serving in a stripey outfit, doing community service.

Sitting in one of the wooden cubicles, Philo said to Birrick, "Where are you from?"

"I am unsure," said Birrick. "It seems like a long time." A silver tray bearing two steaming mugs came flying towards them, its wings flapping, and a gooseneck extending from the front. Settling on the table, the wings and neck disappeared.

"Hmm," said Philo. "We're still short of toffee, otherwise I would get you some. They serve secrets and soda as well, sometimes even food. Where are you going then, Birrick?"

"Well," Birrick paused, "if I get there, home that is, then I will have done my best. I won't be a drongo or pawn. We will see."

"I'll show you the sleeping quarters soon; where we stay when there are late-night meetings. Drink up, perhaps the time is right for us. We will have a say in what goes on now. What is your position in elfdom, Birrick?"

"Befriender, I am a friend. And what is yours?"

"Right now, it's to try persuading the government to sort out the mess we're in."

"Is that what you want? Is that it?" asked Birrick.

"Yes and no. I also want to redress the balance of power, and to avert disaster. These are troubled times. We need a voice in government. With that, we have a key to power, and a key to serve. There is more to come tomorrow. Now we need to rest. You, Birrick, have the silver key. With this, you can be of assistance. You can cross your key with mine. Tomorrow I will take you around the Citadel."

"I've seen the Dark Dreamer," said Birrick. "Have you?"

"Yes," said Philo, putting down his mug. "What happened in your dream?"

"He offered me power in exchange for obedience."

"Did he want you to give him anything?"

"Some stones I had, and my free will. What did he say to you?"

"I was asked," said Philo, "to surrender the services of elves to the power of dreams, which I could not do. After all, even elves have a right to escape slavery. Would you like me to get you a secret from the bar? You have the look of someone searching for secrets."

"How do you know? What is this look?"

"Your ears wag a little when you talk. A sure sign of a person after something."

Philo got up and went to the bar. When he returned he handed Birrick a sealed brown envelope. On the front, the envelope read, 'Top Secret!'

"What do you want in return, Philo?" Birrick queried.

"Fair play, really, and a fair friend."

Saying that Philo took his golden key, and held it to his nose. "Now, let's go," he said, and they sneaked out of the bar, without another word.

Birrick took the envelope and put it in his inside pocket. As he left, he looked up at an elk's head mounted over the exit. He swore that he could see it blinking at him, and its antlers swivelling in their sockets.

Chapter Sixteen

"Ssshh!" whispered Philo. "The quarters are in the attics. We must go quietly to avoid disturbing the Bogle who lives in the hall. Here, up the side staircase."

Philo and Birrick clambered up a narrow stairway, coming to a series of interconnecting halls and passages. A further spiral staircase twisted upwards, seeming to vanish into the ceiling.

"Up there?" Birrick asked.

"That's right. Keep your eyes fixed on the ceiling."

Birrick went first and quickly became breathless with exertion.

"Keep going," urged Philo. "Can you see the large carving of a reindeer in the wood? When you can touch it, press the nose, hard. Then you can enter the elves' quarters."

"It's too high up," said Birrick. "I can't reach it."

"Try to stand on tiptoe, and be quick. We don't want the Hairy Hall Boggart coming after us."

Birrick, in one fantastic stretch, reached out, then jumped and managed to press the nose of the ornate ceiling carving.

"Veni, vidi, dormi," said Birrick. The carving slid to one side, revealing an opening from which hung a rope ladder. "Oh no," said Birrick.

"Oh yes," said Philo, coming up behind him. "I'll go first to help you." Philo, with quick agility, swung his way up the ladder, leaping into the dormitory. Turning to stare down at Birrick, he said, "Come on, friend."

Birrick managed to climb up, without looking down. Taking Philo's outstretched hand, he scrambled into the sleeping area. Standing up, Birrick clapped eyes on a large life-size portrait of a large hairy creature, not quite a man, not quite an ape, but with a tail, glowing red eyes, shining white teeth. Birrick came closer to get a better look.

"Who or what is that?" he asked Philo.

"That's a picture of the Hairy Hall Boggart. You might see him for real if you're unlucky enough. Take any bed you like. Here, this is for you." Philo held out a packet. "It's toffee," he said.

"Thanks," said Birrick, and took it.

"We generally get our rations here, in the Citadel, but it isn't always the same out there in the Present Lands. There have been reports of people queuing for food in Carlion, and some of the other towns. We have a big day ahead of us. What happens will be broadcast everywhere. We all know that Lamguin is in hiding. We have to maintain good magic, good sense, and good government."

"And the divisions of power will allow elves to be important?"

"They must. We have had wars, we have had dark times, the Wall, the rule of academics even. The White Beast was in control for a while. He is trying again to gather his friends around him."

"Why was he removed from power?"

"He tried to insist on the supremacy of science without laws, ethics, or rules. He ate human flesh, ruled by fear, and sought to outlaw magic. Well, we need science, but we need magic too. The White Beast tried to make time go backwards, it wasn't progressing. Nor would he protect the natural laws of nature."

Knock, knock.

"Did you hear that?" asked Birrick.

Knock, knock.

"There it is again." Birrick glanced up at the portrait on the wall. It was empty, the Boggart wasn't there. A hairy creature jumped onto the bed where Birrick was sitting. Its eyes glowed a brilliant orange.

"You have wakened me," said the Boggart, "and now, you must feed me. Give me your toffee, or perhaps I will eat your heart first!"

"But…er…I'm an elf."

"Yes, you'll do, tasty, young, succulent elf. What could be better!"

Birrick stared in horror at the Hairy Boggart who was advancing towards him. The strange eyes changed from orange to yellow to red, its tongue hanging out of its horrible mouth.

Moving quickly, Birrick darted behind an old chair, "Catch me," he taunted.

The Boggart growled, then turned to grab Philo by the hair. Putting a hand around Philo's neck, the Boggart called out, "Save your friend." It started applying pressure to Philo's larynx, and Philo gasped, struggled. His face started to turn purple.

The Boggart was taller than Philo or Birrick. Thinking quickly, Birrick pulled a sheet from a spare bed, then looped it around the Boggart's neck, so that he could pull the Boggart backwards and down. Letting go of Philo, the Boggart fell with a thud. Philo and Birrick sat on top of the creature, trussing him with the sheet as they did so.

"Now what?" said Philo to Birrick.

"We could hang him; I don't feel sorry for him in the least bit."

"Or we could smother him?"

"Send him back to the picture, to where he belongs. Do it with a binding spell, so that he is bound to stay there."

"Do you know how?" Philo asked Birrick.

"Sing with me," said Birrick. "Diablo servus, in pictor captivus, nocte, nigre, furcifer tenemus."

A strong wind went through the room, and there was a loud bang, like the sound of thunder. The sheet lay empty. The two elves turned to the picture, the Boggart was there, bound in chains, with a look of fury on his face.

"Serves him right!" said Birrick.

"I didn't know that spell," said Philo. "You did that well."

"Oh, I can do a few tricks. What's that sound? Sounds like the footsteps of a crowd."

"It's probably the other elves. They come up here too. We have a lot ahead, so now let's sleep."

Philo and Birrick crawled into their separate beds, to wait for what would come in the morning.

A window let in a little light from the stars; Birrick turned his back to the picture of the Boggart, although he still sensed the creature fuming, stewing in its chains. Then Birrick heard another noise. "Mr Unreal?" Birrick wondered.

"The White Beast and the Dreamer will try to enter the Citadel in the next few days. They will try to usurp power. You will have to stop them."

"How can I?" Birrick asked out loud.

"You must use magic. You must gather the others, you will know them. You will work together."

Mr Unreal was quiet again. Birrick sat up in the silence, realizing the position he had been placed in. How would he ever get to the Other World now? What would have happened if he had stayed in the garden of Malloway House? Turning the problem over in his mind, he fell back into his bed and had a night of troubled sleep.

Chapter Seventeen

In Birrick's dreams, Philo came to him to quiz him further.

"What do you want Birrick, in the way of rights for elves?" Philo put the question to him, in his dream state, while the words appeared in white on a black background, in Birrick's mind. In reply, Birrick put his ideas into Philo's dream, "I want an end to elf slavery, equal pay for elves, and properly designated heritage sites for elf magic."

"Well done," replied Philo, "and what shall we suggest concerning our problems with fortune tellers?"

"Give them a proper qualification. Also, I think, there should be rules against driving elves mad or eating elf-flesh. We need to protect our sanity, and our rites, including our rite of passage into adult elf hood."

Philo turned in his sleep, falling out of bed onto the floor, bang. Opening his eyes with shock, there was his fellow elf Birrick, already awake and polishing his medal. Philo immediately felt annoyed at not being first up. Philo wanted to be first in everything.

"Did you have that dream?" Philo asked Birrick.

"Yes, I did," replied Birrick. "Where's breakfast?"

"In the Coven Bar. If we're lucky, you'll meet the government soothsayer. He sometimes says a word or two of warning." Philo jumped up, performed his morning stretch, then said, "Quickly, let's go downstairs. Leave the other elves sleeping. We need to make our plans."

Birrick looked around him at the other beds where sleeping elves lay.

"We can manage without them," said Philo, "for now. They will follow later." Philo pressed on a raised button carved in the wooden floor, and the secret opening yawned wide. Philo and Birrick climbed down the rope ladder, then ran down the stairs to the bar where breakfast was being served.

Once seated in the bar, Philo got out his pen, pad, and magnifying glass.

"Why the magnifier?" asked Birrick.

"So that I can decipher the secret code that I write in." Philo looked up and pointed, "Look, there's breakfast." A silver tray complete with wings and a goose head was flying towards them, laden with toast, porridge, and mugs of hot chocolate. The tray gently came to land on their table.

"Tuck in," said Philo. "After breakfast, we have a further meeting with Lugh and Bede. Then later today, a broadcast will be sent out."

"You mean there will be media publicity? Will we get a makeover?"

"No, we're elves. We get a takeover, and we are the takeover."

"Who is that?" asked Birrick, as a large man with an elephant's head was walking towards them.

"That's the government soothsayer, Victor Ganesh. Hi, Victor!'" called Philo. The large man sat at their table, taking in the partnership between the two elves, and looked at Birrick with large grey eyes.

"Birrick," asked Victor, "why are you an elf?"

"Why are you asking?" said Birrick.

"As an elf, you have a purpose. What is your purpose?"

"To do good."

"And how do you propose to do good here, Birrick?"

"Through friendship," replied Birrick.

"Do you think that will be enough?" asked Victor. "Won't you need something more than that?"

Birrick shivered suddenly, then replied, "That's why I am here, to see if our campaign can succeed. If it can't, then we will think of plan B. We can always have a plan B or even a plan C. How can I get some more hot chocolate?" Birrick turned to Philo. Philo waved at the stripey witch behind the bar. Immediately, she sent another flying silver tray, carrying more hot chocolate their way.

"Strange," said Philo and put his right index finger into his right ear. "Yes, now I hear it. Wait while I tune in." Philo closed his eyes, leaving one finger in his auditory canal. Birrick watched, amazed as Philo sat nodding, grinning, and eventually opening his eyes, removing his finger, and picking up his fresh hot chocolate. Taking a sip, Philo said, "That was my girlfriend."

"Girlfriend?" Birrick looked at Philo with interest.

"Yes…erm…Angelica, a tree elf. She is responsible for the care of the trees in the forest, the Forest of Angaron which surrounds the Citadel. I will see her later. Drink up, it's nearly time for our meeting."

Speedily, the two downed the last of their meal, while the elephant head soothsayer, Victor watched them, silently blinking, waving his trunk, and chewing on a tough banana. After the last of the toast and hot chocolate were gone, wiping away the residue, the two left to climb the staircase to the floor of the high offices within the Citadel.

"Watch out for rats," said Philo. "We have them here sometimes."

Mounting the stairs, Birrick was a little fitter and faster than Philo. Hearing a very loud squeal, Birrick looked for the source, and there at his feet was a large grey rat. Its tail was trapped under Birrick's boot. Lifting his foot, the rat squeaked again and ran off. As they approached, the door to the high office swung open, already seated at the large table were Lugh and Bede, this time without their wigs. Lugh stood up as Philo and Birrick walked through the door.

"Welcome," said Lugh. "You have crossed the threshold into the office of power. Show me your key."

Philo picked up his golden key, holding it aloft. Birrick held up his silver key.

"Interesting," said Lugh, "and who is this, with the silver key?"

"I am Birrick, a friend."

"This other elf," queried Lugh, "is he an advisor?"

"Yes," replied Philo. "Advisor, counsellor, aide, and friend. I need him here."

"Well, as we all hold a key, we are all on an equal footing, so he can stay. Sit down."

As they sat, the bats lifted away from the windows and the sun shone in, haloing Lugh's blonde curls, giving him an angelic look. Bede was bald, with a tonsure. His pate glowed in the sunlight. He wore a priest's robe, with a chain of coloured beads on which he dangled a gold key. Swinging the beads, which were many colours of amber, Bede cleared his throat.

"Let us begin," said Bede, then he sneezed. "Sorry, I've been swimming at the Fortune Fountain and caught a chill. We must discuss government, we need to settle policies, then we must meet with the media to make a news release. Now, let's sit down and discuss the future of the Present Lands and the Citadel."

Lugh, Philo, and Birrick promptly settled onto their chairs. Philo got out his pen, notebook, and magnifying glass, he was ready to talk.

"I would like to raise the problem of prophecy. We have too many prophets making a living telling stories; false prophets. We have to put a stop to this," said Bede.

"Yes, all well and good, but how do you propose to go about this?" Philo asked.

"We need to run a college for divination so that the various forms of soothsaying can be regulated. The government soothsayer trained abroad. We need a similar system here. We must make people qualify reasonably. There have been some ridiculous prophecies lately, including a suggestion that we all ought to turn vegetarian, otherwise we might turn into gnomes! Ahem!"

"And spell casting rites," said Lugh. "That's a problem. Some of the more serious forms of magic should only be performed in special places at certain times of the year. No good going out just because it's a new moon."

"What about elf rites?" asked Birrick.

Lugh's eyes started to gleam. "We will introduce a method of graduation for elves so that on leaving school successful candidates will have their certificate and license."

"And the Academics, what about them?" asked Philo.

"We must limit their control and access to the popular press and literature. We can't have science-gone-mad coming into the public domain. The Academics think they can assert power through science, any science, even unethical science."

"Have you given any thought to the group supporting the White Beast?" asked Philo.

"He did us damage and tried to stir up conflicts to grab power, as did his friend, the Dark Dreamer. We must prevent them from taking the conscience of our times. This is the Present Lands, this is what we have snatched from the past. We must not return to a time when megalomaniac liars tried to destroy what peace we had. Everything must go through a government editing office before entering the public domain. This is our time, we rule through the written word, the press, the conscience of our times." Bede wiped the perspiration from his brow as he finished talking. "I have notes here," he continued. "Any questions?"

Philo passed his notebook to Bede. "Here are our suggestions. Take my magnifying glass, it will decode the secrets for you. What shall we say to the press?"

"We are a coalition; humans, and elves. We will leak the details through a government mole. Our pictures will appear in the 'Daily Augur' tomorrow."

There was a crash, a splintering of glass, then a bang. A large stone, wrapped in a piece of paper landed on the table.

"Weird," said Lugh, lifting the rock and unwrapping it. "We will struggle with you. You will be overcome, or we will be done," read Lugh. He put the paper on the table.

"Can I?" asked Birrick, taking the sheet and reading it. He felt a wave of coldness come over him.

A large bell sounded, ding dong, eleven times, reminding the people of the Citadel that it was time for a break.

Philo turned to Birrick. "In the mirror, friend," he said. They left the office to check their looks in the hall mirror. As they stared at themselves in the glass, Lugh towered above the others, rubbing his hands with a gel through his blonde hair.

"Well, you don't need to comb your hair," Philo said to Bede.

Bede nodded, saying, "I hear footsteps" and turned around. Approaching them was a man, wearing a multi-coloured bow tie. "Dunstan," said Bede, "have you got your camera?"

"Yes," replied the tall bow-tied photographer, taking it out of his shoulder bag. "I want you here, in front of the arched window, where the light is good."

"We will release our policies later," said Bede. "After the photographs, can I entertain you with some magic, over a hot drink?" Dunstan laughed and agreed.

"While you are posing, I would like you two taller men, Bede, and Lugh, at the back with your backs to the window." Posing in the sunlight, there was a large green plant at the side. Birrick brushed right up against it.

"Smile please," said Dunstan. "And again, twice for luck. The originals stay with me, copies go to you and the press. That's it, all done."

"Come with me," said Bede, and the two walked off, followed by Lugh.

Birrick watched as a government mole in a black velvet jacket scurried after them .

"Now Birrick," said Philo, "We have to go talk to the other elves. Let's get going."

130

Philo walked off.

"Help!" cried Birrick.

"What's wrong?" asked Philo turning.

"It's this plant. I'm stuck." The large pot plant had wrapped its ferny tendrils around Birrick's legs so that he could not move away. The more he struggled, the tighter the plant held on. Birrick could feel his circulation slowing as more tendrils wrapped their way around his body, all the way up to his neck.

"Philo, do something!" he cried.

Philo felt in his pocket and closed his fingers around an old mother-of-pearl pen knife. Taking it out, he started to hack at the stem of the plant. A green sap-like fluid rushed from the stalk. Slowly, the fronds released their grip, and Birrick pushed the plant over in his eagerness to get away from it.

Birrick felt shaken, and Philo peered at him. "There's a mark on your neck where that green vampire had hold of you. Angelica won't like this. She is really into ecology, tree, and plant rites. I'll have to get her to give it some healing later."

"But why? It could have killed me?"

"Yes, but it's a plant."

"I knew a vampire once," said Birrick thinking of Dracul. "I never met a green vampire before."

"How did you meet him?"

"In my quest. This is the final part, the Guardian brought me here to meet you."

"Before?"

"Before I can go back home. I am here for now, at least."

"We will go to the forest tonight," said Philo. "Now to the Hall of Elves."

Chapter Eighteen

In the high vaulted hall, the other fifty jacketed, pointy-eared, felt hatted creatures were singing of the good times they all hoped would return. "What will we do without our daily? We sing and dance, rejoicing gaily, now we hope to swell our bellies, eat chocolate toffee every morning! Hooray! Here comes Philo, with this friend. We'll make the by-laws, eat and drink, make secrets indoors. We have high hopes of making law-lords, in the Coven down our pudding, light and tight, time, here we come!"

"Friends, friends," said Philo, moving to the front of the room. Immediately, the whole group gave Philo a standing ovation, as he took the rostrum with Birrick sat at his side.

"Good day to you my fellows!" shouted Philo, raising his hand for silence. "I have attended a meeting with a representative from the Tower of Laws and the Tower of Keys, Lugh and Bede. A triumvirate has been declared, a coalition of equality between elves, monks, and lords. I have the key to the office. Our next duty is to come forward with further ideas to be considered by the triumvirate. Here is the elves' box, write any suggestion which you can think of and put it in here. We, the coalition, have had a media release through the government photographer and mole. Soon, you will be able to read all about it in the press. At this moment, the Law Lords, Lugh and Bede are leaking secrets through the government mole. History marks this date, so to go further, I will give you all an extra round of toffee in the Coven Bar, with any drink you like. We will take the elves' box with us so that you can debate your suggestions before submitting them to the bar."

"Any news of Lamguin the Blade?" shouted out an elf with pink hair.

"No Quentin, but perhaps there will be news soon," replied Philo.

"What about the Angamon Monster? Isn't he a problem as well?" A tallish elf with a red jacket and hat asked the question.

"Darryl put your concerns in the elf box, I will meet you all in the bar."

Philo, followed by Birrick, led the way up a narrow corridor, then turned left, ascending several narrow, steep stone steps. Narrow slit-like openings in the thick walls let in a small amount of light. Philo disappeared around a corner, and Birrick sensed that the air was changing. Taking the corner himself, Birrick stepped out onto an open walkway that ran around the outer walls of the Citadel, giving breath-taking views of green forests, a blue skyline, and undulating hills. A river twisted around one side of the city wall, before snaking off into the forest with a glittering blue bead trail.

Birrick paused to look.

"Hi!" said a voice behind him. Spinning around, Birrick could see Philo leaning over a balustrade and waving to someone below. Philo took a small parcel, wrapped in paper and tied with a string, out of his pocket. Lowering the parcel over the side, a pretty, blonde, elfish figure at the base of the wall took the lowered parcel in one hand, waving back with the other.

"Angelica!" called Philo, as he blew her a kiss. The blonde female waved again, then ran off into the forest. Philo looked at Birrick. "All this is ours," he said. "Isn't it beautiful? And isn't she charmingly pretty? How could we ever give it up? Before the Citadel raven calls three times, and circles the towers, catastrophe will strike. We will find a way to prevent the chaos which could follow."

"Catastrophe? What catastrophe?" asked Birrick, worried.

"It's in the Chronicles, Bede has already told me. We must act tonight and go into the forest. But first, may I enquire, would you give your life to save another or even your fellows?"

"I am an elf," said Birrick, looking squarely at Philo.

"But, if you could?"

Birrick looked out at the forest, at the Citadel walls, at Philo.

"I don't know," he replied, "or perhaps it would depend."

"It is enough," and Philo squinted down at Birrick, patting him on the shoulder. "Come to the bar. There is the business to attend to."

In the Coven Bar, there were many peculiar characters. The soothsayer sat in his corner, the witch in her stripey outfit served behind the counter. A frog who looked quite uncomfortable perched at the end of the bar, next to a sign which read, 'Get your frog legs here'. Lugh, Bede, and the photographer sat at a side table, drinking mead. Two moles were in a cubicle, hotly discussing politics. A large urn stood atop the bar, and every time an elf approached it, it filled up with frothy hot chocolate. The witch, Ursula, dished out toffee shortbread and other victuals.

"What can I do for you?" asked Ursula.

"Well, we'll need food. Have you got any toffee chocolate frogs or mice? We could do with a few of each to get through our next expedition."

Ursula looked under the counter, while the frog hopped about looking sorry for itself.

Raising her head, Ursula said, "Would frog's legs do? Chocolate-coated frog legs?"

The frog atop the counter jumped onto Philo's shoulder.

"What are you doing?" enquired Philo.

"I'm waiting for a princess. Do you know any?" asked the frog. "Also, I'm trying not to become a dinner dish. Try chocolate mice instead, they're far tastier." The frog licked Philo's ear, then hopped off. Philo scratched his head, waiting for Ursula to hand over the requested rations. A quiet came over the noisy bar. Birrick looked around for the reason. There, in the doorway was a tall, slim red-headed woman, in a long green robe, complete with a golden belt and chain.

"It's Roiseen, the Queen of the Elves, why is she here?" Philo turned to bow. Roiseen walked over to the bar and held out her hand.

"As Queen of the Elves, I have come to thank you, Philo. You will be remembered for this."

Philo took her extended hand, kissing the large gold ring which she wore. Turning to Ursula, Roiseen said, "One cauldron of oyster soup, with soda bread and a cup of mead. I will be sitting with Lord Lugh and Bede, over there. Join us, Philo, bring your friend."

The frog leapt up to plant a kiss on Roiseen's forehead. Somehow he bounced off and landed in a cup of hot chocolate.

"A real chocolate frog," Philo laughed, pulling it out and leaving the amphibian on the counter. Ursula handed a large paper bag over to Philo; it had a picture of an elvish design on it.

"Twelve pence to you, and two acorns."

"Oh, here you are," Philo handed over the money, saying, "OK, OK. I know that I'm not being overcharged. Watch out, frog, one day you could find yourself in frog soup. I know where I can get frogspawn, and frogs are not indispensable." The frog looked back at Philo and croaked.

Lugh and Bede made room for the Queen of the Elves, Roiseen. "The time is approaching when we will have to act in our defence."

The photographer looked at her glumly. "Do you have a plan?" asked Roiseen. "Do you know what to do?"

"It depends," said Lugh, "on how they attack or try to take us. The academics are clever, they have access to the forces. We have the chronicles, we have magic, but it depends on cunning, with this we may win."

"And the key, have you given Philo the key?"

"Yes, we have," replied Bede gruffly. "And with Philo, we are in good company, but I'm not so sure about his friend."

"Who is?" Roiseen asked.

"Birrick, the elfin advisor. He seems young, or perhaps short! There they are, the two of them, they're coming over, but I'm not sure whether they know what could be asked of them." Bede stirred his mead thoughtfully with his finger. A cauldron of soup materialized on their table.

"I had a message from Lamguin. It arrived by a falcon." Roiseen looked at the pair, solemnly.

"What did he say?" asked Lugh.

"I have it here." She took a charred piece of parchment out of her robe. Birrick and Philo drew up beside her, to listen quietly. On the paper was a shakily written message, with a red wax seal at the bottom. Roiseen read out, "It will be soon, sooner than you think. When the stars fall from Orion, the worst will come. Only if you can succeed, will order return."

"And how can the stars fall?" asked Lugh, incredulously.

"The comet," said Roiseen. "Orion's comet is coming, any time now. You know this, you have always known this. You, all of you, must act per the chronicles in the defence of the Citadel and the laws of the Present Lands."

"I have not read the 'Book of Last Days and Last Defences' so I am at a loss," replied Lugh. "This last chronicle is, I believe in the library, in the special collection."

"Then read it," answered Roiseen, stroking her auburn hair. "Prepare yourself for what is to come. You have a responsibility Lord Lugh, as do all of you."

Looking at Roiseen's wonderfully aristocratic face, Lugh swallowed, hard. "Alright then, I'm off to read it now. Good day to you, my Queen," said Lugh, bending in a low bow and kissing her gold engraved ring. Taking one last look at the arched eyebrows, high cheekbones, and amber eyes, he turned on his heel, to search the Citadel library for the suggested book. As Lugh was leaving, Bede raised his glass in salute.

"A toast to my lady, Queen of the Elves, and to the safety of the Present Lands." Drinking down his glass in one gulp, Bede excused himself saying, "I must go to attend to our administration. You, Philo, and Birrick, I think you have work left to do. Adieu my lady, adieu. Good health and good luck to you."

With that, Bede excused himself, to leave for the chambers of offices.

Birrick and Philo looked at each other; they looked at the Queen.

"Well," she said, "be prepared. They will be coming, it is in the stars, and I am here, Queen for now, here to tell you. Take comfort in your friendship, in your belief, this will strengthen you both." Her eyes changed from amber back to green. She drew a sign of infinity in the air, with her left hand, then disappeared. She left nothing behind, only an empty bowl of soup.

The soothsayer approached the morose pair sitting at the table.

"There is one thing they are all asking," said Victor solemnly.

"What is that?" asked Philo.

"The DNA. The DNA of Lamguin. Does it match the DNA of the bodies in the crypt? It is not an essential criterion for a ruler, but it is a question. Our leader is supposedly descended from high stock, but no one has asked him to prove this. We have taken his word."

"How can we find out? No one knows where he is?"

"Well, perhaps there is a way. It's not important really. He will reappear when he feels he is safe. You will ask him."

"We will?"

"Yes, it is part of your work to smooth the process of government. As for myself, I simply predict things." The soothsayer blew a ring of smoke over the two friends, from his trunk. "You will be needed, but if you are so able, will we need him?"

"What, Lamguin?" asked Philo, astonished. "Of course, we need Lamguin. He is our figurehead, our leader."

"Yes, but you are our elfin leader, even those pointy ears could carry a crown." The soothsayer blew another smoke ring, and with a wave of his trunk left them alone. The elf with pink hair came up to them.

"We have posted our worries in the box. Now it is your turn to read them." Depositing the wooden voting box in front of Philo, Quentin, the pink punk-haired elf, shrugged his shoulders and danced a jig while a fiddler played a tune on an old violin.

Chapter Nineteen

Lugh found his way to the old oak chamber which was the Citadel library. Row after row of tall bookcases crammed full of old tomes, some very old, some bound in leather, some bound in a ribbon. There was a desk at the front of the main library reception. Sitting there was an old woman, with grey hair, a beard, and a pipe in her mouth, typing away on an old-fashioned typewriter.

Lugh approached the old crone, clearing his throat he raised his voice, "Excuse me, are you the librarian? Can you tell me where the 'Book of Last Days and Last Defences' is kept?"

"Do you have a permit? Are you a government member?" asked the old woman sharply.

Lugh held up his key, "I am Lord Lugh, here is my key of the office."

"No, no. That's not what I want. I want to see your library permit. This book is in the special collection, you must show the correct ID first, not just some blessed key!" The old woman tapped her pipe on the desk and frowned.

"Well…er…I have a business card," and Lugh drew out a manilla coloured card, bearing his title in red.

"Oh, very well then," she barked and spat. "Go down the spiral staircase on the left, the special collection is behind a wire door at the back. You will need to use the government key. That will get you past the wire door. Then second shelf down, the third book from the left. And remember to put it back when you are finished with it." She spat again and returned to her typing.

Lugh wondered where he had last seen as ugly a woman, and with his hand on his gold government key, he squeezed past many bookshelves, until he could see a seemingly endless dark spiral staircase down which he would have to descend.

Gingerly, putting one foot in front of the other, on what was a rattling metal spiral of steps, Lugh saw a strange light in the gloom. At the bottom of the staircase, was standing what looked like a young woman, her hands held high. However, instead of fingers, the hands tapered into waxen candles, which were burning brightly with orange flames. Reaching the bottom, Lugh said, "Hello there" to the young woman, but she gave no reply, simply staring. Putting out a hand to touch her cheek, Lugh inhaled a sharp breath. She was cold, hard, made of wax.

There were several desks, with lamps, some velvet-covered seats, and behind all this a wire cage-like door, behind which were more books. On the door was a sign in red and white which read, 'Private, privileged access only'. Lugh took out his key and tried it in the lock, it creaked, then swung open easily. Edging his way between the shelves, Lugh looked for a slim red bound volume. Bending down to look, among the many black or brown covered books was one red book, with glittering gold lettering on the spine. Lugh stretched out his hand to retrieve it. As he withdrew it, there was a small puff of dust and a smell of mould. Settling at a desk, Lugh opened the book and started to read.

Later that day, as the sun started to set on the Citadel, Birrick and Philo left the walls of government to venture into the Forest of Angamon. They were carrying rations and had in mind a plan. Angelica was due to meet them at the Unkelton Stone, a large boulder left in the forest at the time of the Ice Age. Walking between the Yew Trees, Birrick felt an air of solemnity as the light filtered through the branches of oak, yew, and elm. The last motes of light penetrated the thick forest, and there suddenly, she was. Small, blonde, petite, wrapped in a wool shawl, and sitting on a large uneven rock. Angelina leapt up and ran to Philo, throwing her arms around his neck.

"Philo, you're here! And thank you for my present, look I'm wearing it!" She took off the wool shawl and started to wave it in the air gaily. "Philo my sweet, have you brought me the rations? I'm desperate for a bit of something different. I've been eating acorns and cress sandwiches all day. These trees take quite a lot of pruning, and sometimes they complain to me. One of them, an older oak, told me to fix my problems, before trying to cut back on his. They do get grumpy, expecting all sorts of favours."

Birrick laughed at her. It was, he realized, a magic forest. Philo handed some toffee treats to Angelica.

"Yum," she scoffed the toffee greedily. "There is a rumour in the forest," continued Angelica, "that the Academics have a hideaway here, though I don't know quite where. And Lamguin is supposed to be around here somewhere, with the Lords of the Square Table to protect him."

"Perhaps a tree could tell us?" Birrick asked.

"Well, perhaps," said Angelina, looking at Birrick. "I've heard of you, the new advisor, huh? You're going to be in the press release. Well, it could be worse Birrick, have you seen the Bogle?"

"Not yet, are you going to take me to see him?" Birrick replied.

"Well, one year, the Bogle was appointed an advisor, but he didn't last long. Still, he stays there, trapped in the Citadel, just waiting to curse anyone he's lucky enough to come upon. You won't do that!" Angelina looked thoughtfully at Birrick. "For an elf, you must be good, otherwise, you wouldn't be here. Do you want to see the Angamon Tarn Monster? I can show you that."

"Is it far?" asked Birrick.

"No, just this way." Angelica turned in her woollen cloak, proceeding through the trees of the Angamon Forest, singing happily of wild garlic and the taste of caramel toffee.

The stars began to appear in the sky, but the forest was dark. Angelica seemed to know where she was going, she knew the forest well. A rabbit leapt ahead of her, chased by a fox. A new sound, carried on the breeze reached her. Stopping, she stood still, silently listening. Waving to the other two, she ducked under a low branch, then crawled on all fours, positioning herself behind some broom bushes. Putting a finger to her lips, she beckoned Birrick and Philo. They joined her. Parting a broom bush branch, Angelica could see a crowd of men and women, grouped around one much taller man. As he bowed down to his friends, Angelica could see a red birthmark on his bald head, in the shape of a pi symbol.

Drawing himself to his full height, the tall man, dressed in white, spoke out.

"Friends, academics, all of you, we are here to promote our interests, science, and philosophy. Yes, even anarchy. We are the rightful leaders for our times, and the Present Lands. We must take control of the Citadel, and back at HQ, the Dreamer is preparing himself. In his methods, there's some chance of success. When the Starmen fall, we will attack the Citadel. We will capture the Tarn Monster and use him for our purposes, for science. There is no going back, with Lamguin in hiding, the time is now. The leadership of lords, monks, and elves is a weak one. Our cold-headed rationality is a greater gift. We will turn our efforts into a media of mind control. Considering the talents of those gathered here, we are fair. With the Dreamer and the Monster to assist us, we will do damage and the dark work we can. We will rule with science, are you with me? If you are, raise your right hand, and shout with me, 'Hail high, hail white, we lead with might'."

"Hail, hail, hail!" shouted the crowd. "Hail, hail, hail! We are right, we lead with might, on this dark night. Hail!"

"And now, to the Angamon Tarn. We must act quickly." The tall man in white jeans and a white jumper, lead his crowd directly past the broom bushes where the elves were crouching. Angelica stayed low down, out of the eye level of the crowd. She knew that any movement might betray them. Once the crowd had gone, Angelica turned to the other two.

"The rumours are true."

"And the tall bald man?" asked Birrick.

"That's the White Beast," replied Angelica. "He is strong here, Philo. What shall we do? What shall we do?"

Philo looked at Angelica, then looked into the clear night sky. A large bird flew past, calling, "Caw, caw."

"A raven." Birrick looked at Philo. "A raven, but it only called twice. We must get to the monster before they do and before the raven calls for the third time."

"Or?" asked Birrick.

"Or we could be too late. Can you take us to the tarn Angelica before the Academics get there?"

"Well," said Angelica, closing her eyes momentarily. "Perhaps we could go by wisp. I could try to call one for us. A wood wisp, some of the trees might oblige."

Angelica put her hand to Philo's face, then walked up to a large, gnarled oak tree, climbing up it and sitting in the crooked branch fork. Holding out her arms up high, she called out in a sing-song high-pitched voice, "Weep! Oh wisp, a call to thee, I beg you come from within your tree. Leave the safety of this oak, protect us with your magic cloak. Take us quickly, where we seek, to help the monster in the deep." As she finished, she closed her eyes, drawing her hands down over her face, then turning to the knot in the tree.

"Why should I help you, why should I give you my wisp?" The tree spoke angrily.

"We must avert disaster. We need your help, please. We need to get to the tarn quickly and without being seen. We want to preserve the peace in the forest."

"Very well then," moaned the oak, and a pale green spirit slowly emanated from the knot. Angelica jumped down from the oak and picked up a fallen branch from the forest floor. It still had some leaves.

"Hold tight to this boys. The spirit will envelop us. The branch will keep us together."

The greenwood wisp surrounded them as they held onto the branch, raising them high above the forest trees.

Speeding through the air, a voice whispered to Birrick, "Don't look down." Following the course of a dark stream, which led to the tarn, the trees passed by in a carpet of shadowy murmurings. Philo could see the Angamon Tarn ahead, a beautiful oval of unbroken midnight blue, unbroken except for a large, pointed rock that protruded from the water. The smooth glass-like surface rippled, and a small head emerged from the waters, extending beyond the tarn on a long scalene neck.

Angelina and Birrick watched in silence as the scaley small head drew level with Philo.

"Yes," asked the monster. "What do you wish? Why have you come to disturb me from my one hundred years of sleep? It was just a brief nap. I meant to go on sleeping for another five hundred years!"

"We've come to help you away. You are in danger," replied Philo.

"Danger, me? No." The monster yawned and started to submerge.

"Oh please!" said Birrick. "Quick, let's land the wisp." So down they descended until they were standing beside the tarn.

"No one can hurt me, a monster, surely?" said the monster. "Or at least, no one has managed to hurt me yet!"

"The Academics want you. They want to capture you and use you for their cause; the cause of science, the cause of cruelty." Birrick looked up at the monster, feeling quite worried.

"The Academics are planning to take over the Citadel, and they plan to ensnare you," said Philo. "The White Beast is with them; they are on their way here now."

"Where should I go?" asked the monster. "Where could you hide an animal my size?" He blinked, then stared at Philo.

"Come with us," said Angelica. "We will find a way, but there isn't much time. You can give us a ride. We don't weigh much. Just don't eat us until you're safe." Philo kicked Angelica as she spoke.

"I'm vegan. I only eat leaves and weeds."

"I need to get back to the woods," murmured the wisp. "You can take them from here." Slowly, the green wisp diffused itself between the trees and disappeared.

Chapter Twenty

"Quick, we must leave before the third call of the raven," said Philo. "Are you coming with us or are you waiting for the Academics? Come with us, before disaster can strike."

"Ho, you with the big nose and pointy ears, you talk like an elf. I prefer your pretty friend. I'm happy to give her a lift. Where are we going, my dear?"

"Well…er…you have to take all of us, and we will hide you on the other side of the Citadel, in a secret place. Will you take us all?"

There was a pause, the monster looked seriously at the three elves. "Well, well, or very well. I have to take you at your word I suppose. We'll all go together then. Although, I would like to go back to sleep."

"Come on," said Philo. "Be quick, come out of the tarn and we will climb onto your back."

The large, clumsy body, legs, and tail of the tarn monster waded onto the shore so that the elves could climb up his tail, onto his back. "Come on," he said. "It may be damp, and you need a head for heights."

As Birrick climbed up last of all, he started to fear slipping off the moist scaley skin. Holding on tight to Angelica, who held on tightly to Philo, who held on tightly to some strands of hair that cascaded down the creature's neck, Birrick closed his eyes tightly.

"To the secret side of the Citadel, on the northern wall, we will be in the shadows there, safe for a while. Vamos," cried out Philo. The monster unfolded its wings, made a short run, then took off. Tucking its webbed feet and unattractive legs beneath it, it spiralled upwards, away from the tarn, and forest. As the four flew off in the night sky, a dark bird flew low over the tarn, calling "Caw, caw, caw."

"The raven," said Angelica. She looked back and could see a crowd of people gathering by the side of the tarn, one of them a very tall man with a bald head.

"So much for train travel. I prefer this, the monster mash, and I suppose we will have to find some monster munch as well," Philo called out quite exhilarated.

"The White Beast is down there with his friends," said Angelica.

"So much for him then," said Philo.

The tall bald man they called the White Beast, stood at the edge of the tarn, his followers around him.

"Take the chemical mixture and pour it into the tarn," commanded the leader of the Academics. "If we drug the monster, he will do as we wish."

"But look over there, look under the sign of Orion, can't you see?" The dark woman pointed up at the sky. Following her gaze, the Beast could see the monster. A meteor shower started to fall from Orion's Comet, so that the stars shone luminescently, falling to the ground from the night sky.

"The Starmen are coming. We must go back to Arcadia H.Q., our place of safety. Drew and Drake, you shall complete the second stage of our plan. You will go on to the Citadel. We will return to our hideaway. There is time, we still have the cover of darkness for a few hours yet. Remember, do not tell anyone where we are, or what we are at, on pain of death."

"On pain of death?" asked Drew, raising his eyebrows quizzically.

"On pain of death," said the Beast. "I will see to it personally. Now go, be sure to succeed in what you do."

"We will follow our instructions to the best of our ability," said Drake, the taller, thinner of the twins, a man with a plaited beard. "How shall we introduce ourselves at the Citadel gates?" asked Drake.

"Say that you are visiting friends. "Remember, only drink from your bottle, not the fluid solution, it is drugged." As the green eyes of the Beast bored into Drake's and then Drew's, "Remember," he said again quietly. The three clasped hands in a three-thumbed handshake. Then the Beast with the others made for the near side of the forest, where they had transport; Drew and Drake turned in the direction of the Citadel.

Lugh sat in the library, pouring over the 'Book of Last Days and Last Defences'. The time had passed, but he read on, and as he read on, he became increasingly worried by what he read. The book clearly stated that in the later days of the Citadel, the last defence would be in the mind. It would take a very strong mind to withstand the shadows, the cravings, the poisoning that power could bring. The only real defence, according to the record, would be through the movements of an innocent newcomer. Someone strong, young, and pure enough to repel the cravings of this world, the Present Lands, and lead the Citadel away from the chaos to order. The need for harmony with nature, magic, and science and to rule in peace being of utmost importance. After all, what is the good in trying to bend the laws of the universe for personal gain? Try as Lugh might, he could not find the name of the newcomer in the text, nor discover whether they would be; man, lord, monk, or elf! Wondering what to do about it and scratching his head, Lugh looked out of the library basement window. There was the comet in the night sky, the meteor shower a very brilliant sight of yellows, oranges, and golds. Lugh put the book back and went to the Coven bar for a final nightcap. While drinking his mead in the bar, the official soothsayer came up to him and said, "May I?" The elephant-headed man sat at the table beside him, his trunk wrapped around a banana milkshake.

"It's the last night," said the soothsayer, Victor, looking seriously at Lugh.

"Last night for what?" asked Lugh, impatiently glaring at the elephant head.

"It's the last night of the full moon, and the last chance for innocent encounters, well, for a while anyway. There will be trouble. Here, flip a coin, heads you win, tails I win."

"No thanks, that's just too much like chance."

"Chance will come your way," said the soothsayer, and finishing his drink, he left.

At the main gate to the southern wall of the Citadel, Drew and Drake stood arguing over who should go first. "I think you should go first, Drake. You're taller and stronger," said Drew. Drake stroked his plaited beard, saying, "No you go first, Drew. You're quicker." The two were twins, but easy to tell apart due to Drake's strange beard. Drake paused, felt in his pockets, then approached the gate at which a watchman stood guard.

"Let us pass," said Drake.

"What's the purpose of your visit?" The chubby watchman who took up most of the entrance raised his mismatched eyes to look Drake in the face.

"We are here to see friends," Drake replied.

"Very well, what's the password?" asked the gatekeeper.

"Malarmia," said Drake. The watchman took out a notebook with a list of passwords to check.

"Oh, yes, you can pass. Through you go." Standing aside, the watchman let the twins through the walls of the Citadel, not knowing what would follow.

Moving into the first plaza, Drake pointed to a well on the left. "Over there," he whispered. The two silently approached the stone-walled well.

"Only half," said Drew. Drake took out a blue bottle, pouring some of the contents into the well.

"Now, for the second well. It's in the North Plaza, behind the halls. I think we go this way." Drake carefully twisted the top on the bottle, secreting it in his large poacher's pocket. Drake took the lead in escorting Drew along a narrow-cobbled street where the buildings seemed to lean towards each other. A tall blonde man turned the corner and clapped eyes on Drake and Drew, it was Lugh.

"Excuse me," said Drake, "is the North Plaza this way? How can we find it?"

"Follow this street to the fountain, turn left, go through the main marketplace, and directly in front of you is Zoffany Street. It leads to the North Plaza, there is a well there. Also, some of the hotels will still be open. You can buy a meal at one of them should you wish."

"We are visiting friends near the North Plaza, thank you. We don't need a hotel," replied Drake. Lugh looked at them, shrugged his shoulders, and went off to the Lord's quarters where he would spend the night. Lugh felt uneasy, he expected to meet with Philo again, and Bede in the morning. The arrival of the elvish queen and his time in the library left him a worried man. Also, a rumour had reached him, that Lamguin, should he return, would be asked to prove his credentials through his DNA. This had been one of the ideas put forward in the elves' suggestion box.

Drake and Drew paced on through the dimly lit streets of the Citadel at night. Coming to an opening, there was a beautiful fountain, with many multi-coloured lights shining on the heads of mermaids, the tails of fish, and the music of the sirens played in the background. Drew stopped to stare. There was a group of merrymakers outside a tavern, "Don't you want to go in?" asked Drew.

"Ssshh!" replied Drake. "Let's be nimble, let's be quick, no time to give a glass a lick. Over here, look, Zoffany Street, North Plaza this way." An old sign swinging from a rickety lamppost announced the direction which Drake took, through a marketplace and on down another street; Drew a few paces behind him. Drake broke into a run, reaching the North Plaza and the Northern Well first. Taking out the bottle from his large inner poaching pocket, he poured the rest of its contents into the damp well mouth. Drew stepped up beside him, as the well had steps to it. Drake reached out, grabbed Drew by the neck, and threw him down the well. Drew screamed as he fell, the sound echoing out in the cold night. Drake put the bottle away, stalking off and intending to join the rest of the Academics at the headquarters. "Humbug," said Drake out loud and spat on the streets of the Citadel.

Chapter Twenty-One

Bump, bump, bump! The monster came to a rough halt behind the north wall, banging his head and his tail as he did so.

"Wait," ordered Philo. "I will open the hidden quarter, where you will be safe." Philo tapped three times on the north wall, saying, "Porticus abrir." A large hole opened up in the wall. "In there," Philo said to the monster.

"Must I?" asked the scaley creature. "I'd quite like something to eat."

"Well, we can get you some herbs and leaves, but you should wait inside. The Academics will never find you there."

"Oh, all right, but call me by my name please, 'Jackaw' and I'm particularly partial to ivy leaves."

"Look Jackaw, get in, we will bring you what we can."

Jackaw turned and clambered through the hole until all that was sticking out was his head and neck.

"Sorry," said Jackaw. "You can't cut it off, and I am a strange shape to fit in a hole."

"We'll bring some leaves from the bushes Angelica; you Philo can stay with Jackaw." Birrick and Angelica dawdled off, as Philo called after them, "Be quick."

"The moon is still shining," said Jackaw, "and there is the comet which is meant to tell of great events or strange doings. Do you remember Lamguin?"

"Yes, he's not been long gone, soon he will return, and I believe his heredity will be proven. Who are you related to Jackaw?"

"Aaah, that's a story. Supposedly there is another like me, in a loch far off in Scotland. Though I think the tourists scared him off. He's my second cousin, Nessie. Pollution has scared most of my kind into living far out at sea, in the depths of the oceans where cameras, plastic bags, and tourists generally just don't go. Seaweed isn't a bad diet when it's fresh."

After a few minutes Philo spied Angelica and Birrick returning with some branches of greenery.

"Here we are," called Angelica cheerfully, holding up a branch for Jackaw to chomp on.

"Mmm, delicious." Jackaw smiled for the first time in more than a hundred years.

"Now, don't we have to get back? Aren't there more meetings tomorrow? Won't the gates be closed by now?" Birrick sounded worried as he looked at the other two.

"I know a way," said Angelica. "I know every inch of these walls and I know another entrance."

"Then take us," said Birrick. "We will follow you."

"What about Jackaw?" asked Angelica.

"I'm fine," called out Jackaw, chewing on another leaf.

"It's the old mine entrance. It's still there, it never was filled in. Come with me." Angelica's pointed ears waggled with pleasure as she led them along a narrow earth path, coming to a stop at a gaping mine shaft, a hole in the ground.

Philo looked on in disbelief. "Down there?" he asked.

156

"Yes, look, there's a rope at the other side which we can climb down. Scared?"

"No, just… er… surprised," muttered Philo. Looking unsure of himself, he asked, "Is there anything else down there?"

"Only coal," said Angelica.

"I'll go first," said Birrick. "I've been in a few dark places in the Underworld."

"The what?" asked Philo.

"Oh, you know, I've been underground before now." Grabbing hold of the rope, Birrick lowered himself over the edge of the hole and into the dark mouth.

Pushing his feet against the uneven walls of the shaft, Birrick moved deftly downwards, passing the rope through his hands. Before Birrick had gone fifteen metres, Philo took the rope, starting to lower himself into the earth. Birrick could see the sky in the shaft opening, and Philo's shape, a dark outline against the night stars. Birrick thought that he was strong for an elf, but as he swung down, Philo dislodged a clod of coal which hit Birrick on the head. Temporarily stunned, Birrick slithered down the remainder of the rope, creating a cloud of coal dust as he travelled, swinging now and again into the shaft walls. In his hands, he felt the rope burning him, until, shaken he landed at the bottom, dazed, and hurt. Slowly, Birrick's eyes grew accustomed to the darkness. Wasn't that a movement in the black of the pit?

Taking a few steps forward, Birrick could make out a woman's face with a mane of hair, she was wearing a mask with two eye holes. "I am the Bogle that lives in the hole. I am here to bogle and burgle. What can you give me?" The loud voice that seemed to be coming from a small woman, made Birrick jump.

She came closer, and Birrick could see the painting on the mask. "What can you give me?" This time, Birrick thought he could hear bells. He felt in his pockets, but there was nothing he wanted to give. Another thudding sound made Birrick jump.

"Hi," said Philo, who landed beside Birrick. "Would you like a toffee ration?" Philo held a ration packet out to the woman. "Or perhaps you would like a spell?"

"Give me the toffee and the spell, I am hungry enough." The bogle snatched the packet. "What spell can you give me? Make it a good one."

"Well…er…I can give you a spell for making music, making music so that all who are here around it can give in to your desire. Or perhaps a spell for catching the motes of the moon to weave wishes. Or a spell to provide an endless supply of toffee."

"Right. I'll have all those, one of each, please. Give them to me, now!" The woman barred her teeth and snarled a little, coming almost eyeball to eyeball with Philo, tossing her dark hair.

Taking a small silver penny whistle from his pocket, Philo spoke out, "Magicality, defer calamity, I give you your wish, take these three spells as the whistle knells." Playing a tune on the whistle, three silver magical notes appeared in the air. Dancing around the woman, she took them and pocketed them.

"They'll be of use later," said the bogle. "The stairway is on the right." She moved off to eat her toffee.

"Where's Angelica?" asked Birrick.

"She's gone back to see her mother in the forest. We have to go back alone. She told me the way, up the staircase and turn left." Philo bent almost double to squeeze through a small doorway to the secret staircase. Followed by Birrick, they climbed up shallow steps carved in the rock. There were many faces etched into the walls on either side.

Passing the faces, Birrick thought that they were saying things to him. Then he realized that perhaps this was Mr Unreal, repeatedly warning him, "Look out! there is more to come."

"Go away Mr Unreal, go away. You're on my mind," whispered Birrick out loud.

"Hah, that's where it's all for you, in your mind" replied Mr Unreal. There was a kind of light, coming from the walls, and after a while, Birrick and Philo were standing in the North Plaza. They caught sight of a man running off, and another smaller man, crawling out of the well.

"Back to the elves' quarters?" asked Birrick.

"Yes," replied Philo, "I'm tired."

Chapter Twenty-Two

Drew caught up with Drake, and they ran on out of the south gate, where around a corner of the outer walls, there was a car waiting for them. Getting in the back, the driver barked out, "You're late, and I don't want any mess in my car. You have done the deed?"

"Yes," replied Drake, "we have."

"Good, the monster is in hiding, but we will find him, we need to go back to HQ, and I'm driving so be quiet, I have to concentrate."

"OK Lucas," said Drake, "I can't wait to hear the final part of the plan." Drake smiled to himself, then said to his brother Drew, "Did you get a little wet?" Laughing, Drake closed his eyes, to gather his mental strength.

In a hillside, on the road to Nowhere, on the edge of the Present Lands, there was a barrow, and within the barrow, there was a large room. This room had a stone doorway, a laboratory, a flotation tank, a television screen mounted at the top of one wall. There was a large table where a group of academics sat playing cards and dominoes. Drew and Drake rapped out the signal, rat a tat, rat a tat. The door was pulled back by the beast, it had a metal ring on the inside.

"You're back," said the Beast, "and in good time."

"You have done your work?" A bald man with tattoos approached them. "it is complete?"

"Yes," said Drew. "we have done as much as we could, though we did not find the monster. Now we deserve our reward, what is it to be?"

"Hypnotelepathy," said the bald man, "I will program you through your subconscious, with this we will overcome all obstacles. Go and relax on the beanbags while I prepare myself. Help yourself to a drink of whatever you like. The mini-fridge is over there beside the beanbags."

"And what are you going to do?" asked Drew.

"I am going to prepare my mind in the flotation tank." With that the strange bald man climbed into the tank, attaching wires to tattoos on his head, and starting to float.

Drew and Drake went over to the fridge, inside was a green bottle that read, "Only to be taken internally."

"That'll do," said Drake, pouring himself and his brother a large glass of a minty-smelling drink. Lounging and reclining on the beanbags, as the two sipped from the glass they felt drowsy. As they slept, a green smoke started coming out of their ears. The other academics watched in amazement.

"It's the effect of deep hypnotelepathy," said the White Beast. "It's burning out their brains, their memories, everything. In the morning they will know nothing. Look at the television screen."

On the screen, the Angamon Monster could be seen struggling out of a strange hole in a wall. As he struggled free, he ambled lazily off in search of fresh water and fresh food.

"Now we'll get him," said the White Beast. "he won't get far."

One of the academics sat dealing the cards for a fresh game.

"I have the Ace of Diamonds," said a small brown-haired woman.

"And I have a Joker," said a man in a flat cap.

"The Joker isn't a proper card, or it means misfortune if you try to use it." The woman warned, looking at him mysteriously.

'Who cares about misfortune? Whose side are you on? There is no such thing as luck. '

"There is no such thing as luck," said Philo to Birrick, as he cleaned his teeth and drank down his breath freshener mixed with tap water. "We have the forces to thank for our position and good judgement."

Birrick picked at his mouth with a toothpick and said nothing. Before turning out the light in the Elves' Quarters, Philo smiled at himself in the mirror, and, putting one finger in his ear, he sent a quick telepathic goodnight to Angelica. Getting into bed, he said, "Birrick, sleep well." Promptly his head hit the pillow, he fell into a deep sleep.

As Birrick tossed and turned, many thoughts came to him. He looked at his reflection in a stream, on the stream bed there were many golden coins. Reaching out his hand to pick them, he heard a voice, "Take them and you are mine." Looking up, he could see a shadow, then the shadow formed to show its dark eyes, its tattoos. Birrick started to back away from the stream, but the shadow grew longer, taller. Turning and running at the shadow, Birrick took a huge leap, breaking through the dark image, and landing on the other side of the stream. Walking on a few steps, he opened his hand, there was a gold coin, it was a foil-covered chocolate coin. Birrick ate it, and turned over in bed, hoping for a new dream.

Philo also came to a stream, and he saw Birrick walk off ahead of him on the other side. A tall, bald man held out a sack to Philo. Philo took it, it felt heavy.

"If you take it, you agree to let us in," said the man. Philo looked at the bag, then at the man. "I do not agree," said Philo.

"But you are bound," said the man.

"No, I do not agree." Philo emptied the bag into the stream. "You do not hold me in your hands, I am an elf, I swear by the forces, not by fool's gold, which is all that is. You cannot take us so easily, you will see." So, saying, Philo swam off downstream, leaving the Dark Dreamer with all he could offer behind in the deepest night. And in the Citadel, there were many dreams that night.

Birrick woke early, and he thought immediately that he would check on the Angamon Monster, Jackaw. Climbing to the top of the Citadel, planning to look down the north wall and talk to the monster as its head looked out of its hole, Birrick bent over the parapet, but the monster did not seem to be there. Calling out, "Jackaw, Jackaw." His words had no effect. Then, turning and looking to the south, he could see a large truck with a monster's head poking out, as it trundled off in the direction of H.Q. on the road that led to Nowhere. Birrick put his hand over his eyes, not liking to believe what he could see.

"Yes it's true," said Mr Unreal. "The academics have Jackaw. Do not drink the water, Philo already has, and he will be unable to help you. Go and find Bede, he is in the office.

Philo is drugged, as is anyone who took the tap water. Lugh and Bede only drink mead, they will work with you. Go now, before it gets much lighter, and before more damage is done."

Birrick turned and ran down the flight of stairs into the hallway where the Citadel had its more important offices. The tall door was open, and Birrick could see Bede in deep discussion with Lugh. Clearing his throat, Birrick took off his hat and approached the pair.

"We have been waiting for you" said Bede. "You must go into the forest and find Lamguin. He must be brought here for DNA testing, and to rally the cause."

"The cause?" queried Birrick?

"Yes, we are under attack, listen." Bang, suddenly a large shock wave of noise filled the room, and a mirror on the wall fell onto the floor, splintering into many pieces. "The cause of the Citadel. We need him, Lamguin." Smash, another missile landed in the corridor outside. Bede came up to Birrick and put his hand on Birrick's forehead. "You must go at once; you know a guide?"

"Yes, Angelica," replied Birrick.

"She will take you; she will follow the signs. Good luck my friend, you are charmed."

"Caw, caw, caw, caw," Birrick started as he heard the raven call. Frightened for himself, and also frightened of the future, Birrick ran hurriedly off into the Forest of Angamon.

Walking along in the early morning light, Birrick heard Mr Unreal's voice, "Follow the shining path." Looking down, Birrick could see a trail of granite pebbles that glinted. The path led under many low trees until it stopped at a small pool with a statue in the centre. Birrick bent to put his hand into the water and take a drink. The bottom of the pool was covered in gold coins. As he bent, he heard a voice, "Look hard, look into the water." As Birrick stared into the shallow pond, a face started to form, with tattoos, two very large dark eyes, the cheekbones, the mouth.

"You will go far," said the man, "why don't you jump in?" Birrick felt a strange pull, an attraction to the water, the gold, the tattooed face. Birrick wished to join the man, and free himself of all responsibility. A tattooed hand started to extend from the water, towards him.

"Hi down there," cried out a high-pitched female voice. Birrick turned from the pool. He could see close by a log cabin among the many bushes and trees. One particularly twisted tree grew beside the wooden building. From this tree were hanging a pair of legs in purple socks. Coming closer, Birrick could make out Angelica's face and body attached to the legs. Picking up a stone, he threw it at the window of the cabin calling out, "Angel Angelica, Angel Angelica."

Angelica suddenly appeared through a doorway in the tree.

"Birrick, you're here!" cried out Angelica. "Go inside the cabin and I will join you. Why have you come?"

"The monster Jackaw has gone, the Citadel is under attack, and apparently, the water system has been drugged. Have you seen a bald man with tattoos, the Dreamer? Alongside the Academics, he is trying to get power, control. I have seen him in my dreams."

Angelica laughed, "That old bogey huh? And is it only the water in the Citadel which is drugged?"

"I think so."

"Then not everyone will be affected. I suppose that you are going to tell me that we need to find Lamguin?"

"Yes, how did you guess?"

"I'm not an elf for nothing, and nor are you."

"But no-one knows where Lamguin is!"

"Well, er, perhaps it's just that no-one admits where Lamguin is. I will be down soon. Be polite to my mother," called out Angelica, "she is inside."

As Birrick entered the small cabin, he noticed a small woman with white hair sitting on a couch knitting a very long scarf.

"Good morning," said Birrick uncertainly, "I've come to talk to your daughter."

"Ach, she'll be here soon, just busy picking a few berries outside." The needles clicked away, and Angelica appeared at the door with a basket of red and white berries in her arms.

"Do you know where we are going? Will you take me to him, Lamguin?" Birrick asked Angelica, uncertainly.

"Well, if you come with me, you must be blindfold," said Angelica, "I am bound to secrecy, and no one is supposed to know the way. Do you agree? Agree on pain of death Birrick, if anything goes wrong, we will all pay dearly."

Birrick gulped.

"This place, where we can find Lamguin, if the Lords find that I have given the destination away, I will pay with my life or worse your life. Come here." Angelica took a coarse linen rag and tied it over Birrick's eyes. "Now I have you under my control Birrick, I am tying this rope around your waist so that we will not be parted." She did just this, and Birrick stood, stupefied, as he realized he was in the power of a female, a sensation which was quite strange. He knew that he would have to do just as she said.

Angelica took hold of the other end of the rope and tucked it into her belt.

"What if we have to turn a corner?" asked Birrick helplessly.

"I will give you guidance." Angelica tugged on the rope. "Come on, elves together, let's go." With that she marched out of the cabin, Birrick, blindfolded reluctantly followed behind.

Chapter Twenty-Three

In the Citadel Philo awoke, noted the daylight coming in through the window, and turned over in bed. A dark figure flickered momentarily before his eyes, then disappeared. Philo saw the coins on his bedside cabinet, with a packet of cinder toffee. Breaking open the packet, he bit off a chunk and thought no more of it. He looked for Birrick's sleeping form in the bed next to his, but the bed was empty. Philo went to wash and gargle as part of his early morning routine. Taking his mouthwash with tap water, he swilled the mixture around his mouth, then swallowed. Noticing a few hairs on his chin, he felt proud, washed his face, cleaned his ears, and went off to the Coven Bar.

In the bar, there was already a crowd of elves sitting at a number of the smaller tables.

"Did you see him?" asked a small grey-haired elf, in conversation with his bespectacled friend. "Did you see him in your dreams? Or this morning as you woke up? Was he there for you?"

The sandy-haired elf with glasses replied, "Yes, I did see him, and it's been a long time for me too. I think we're having a vote today. Are you voting for the Dreamer? I think I might. I could let him have a turn, just for a change."

A large thud could suddenly be heard, and the chandelier in the Coven Bar started to shake, jangle, and rotate.

Philo turned to look at his fellows and felt a sense of unease.

"What's your order?" asked the stripey witch behind the counter.

"Sausages and beans," replied Philo, "with a mug of hot milk. Have you seen anyone last night? While you were asleep?" Philo asked the witch.

"What if I have? We have plenty of visitations. Many things or people come in dreams, to the point where I am used to it. There was a shadow in the night, but it means precious little now. Why, did you see anything or anyone?"

Philo retreated from answering, and said, "Make it three sausages please, with toast."

"I'll send it over," said the witch and returned to her stove where the food was cooking.

Philo looked around him, he couldn't see Birrick. Also, he wondered whether the monster, Jackaw, was where they had left him last night. As the tray came flying towards him, carrying his breakfast, Philo picked up his knife, fork, and napkin. Sitting in his usual corner cubicle, he thought he might try to contact Angelica. Putting his finger in his left ear, he tried to tune in. But all he could hear was a fuzzy noise like broken wireless and the talking of the elves around him.

After eating, the sandy-haired elf, Tyrone, got up and approached Philo.

"We are voting?" asked Tyrone.

"Er, yes, I suppose so, but we haven't set up the voting box yet."

"And we are voting for?" Tyrone looked serious.

"We are...er...voting for an advisor, and according to request, the only two candidates we have are...er...the Dreamer," said Philo.

"Yes, or?"

"Or Birrick."

"Who'?"

"Birrick, he was featured in the Daily Augur yesterday, I think. He has been at my side most of the time."

"But only for a day or two. I'll get the voting box," said Tyrone, self-importantly. "I know where it's kept."

Disappearing into a walk-in cupboard, Tyrone reappeared with a large wooden box bearing the mark X. "Here we are," said Tyrone, heaving the box onto the bar. Standing on a table, and clattering his spoons, Tyrone called out, "Hear me, hear me, hear me. Today we have a vote, either for Birrick; a nobody elf who does nothing, or for the Dreamer; whom I feel respect for. I know whom I would prefer, and for whom I will vote, let the casting begin."

Tyrone jumped down, flourished his napkin, wrote the name of his preferred candidate, and put it in the box. With this, he was followed by the other elves.

Philo sat, impressed, and saddened. He realized that he was supposed to vote himself, but his confusion made him hesitate. How could he not vote for Birrick? Eventually, taking a pen, he wrote on a scrap of paper, 'Anonymous' on one side, 'Birrick' on the other, and placed his vote in the box. Even the stripey witch voted, as did several wizards and warlocks in the bar. Philo waited patiently for the outcome to be announced, as a government mole sat counting the votes. A giant television screen hung over the one-armed bandits.

The government soothsayer, Victor, came up to Philo waving his trunk.

"I know the outcome," said Victor. "Disaster will befall us, and soon the Citadel will be overrun."

"Overrun or overruled?" asked Philo.

"Maybe both," said the soothsayer glumly. "Now is a good time to emigrate." The soothsayer looked worried, a frown on his elephant face.

"That won't come surely?" said Philo. Suddenly the big TV screen lit up. "Now we have the outcome of this morning's vote," announced an attractive TV model; a particularly good-looking woman. "The winner of the new position of government advisor is…" She paused, looking at her cue card, "the Dreamer, with one hundred and ten votes out of one hundred and twenty. Nine votes for Birrick, and one vote for Anonymous." Immediately, the Dreamer materialized in the Coven Bar, and hundreds of mice burst out of the skirting boards, scurrying all over the place.

"Friends, how glad I am to be here among you," announced the Dreamer to everyone in the bar. The background conversation which had been going on hushed, all eyes on the dark balding man with tattoos. "Not only am I looking forward to working with you, I wish to champion the cause of my friends about me, also my friends outside the Citadel, the Academics and the Starmen. They feel that their voices must be heard, and I know that you will want to make their acquaintance. Take me to the high office where I can meet with Lugh and Bede."

Philo looked on in disbelief. "Here are my details," said the Dreamer, handing a card to Philo. The bar was plunged into darkness. Philo ran for the main exit, where there was the only light, apart from the television, flickering on and off, and the flashing of the one-armed bandits.

As Philo climbed the stairway to the main chamber of office, the Dreamer hovered behind him.

"This way," said Philo as he turned to take a look at the tattooed man. "They will be waiting for you." As the two climbed the stairs to the upper floors silently, Philo had a feeling of dread, as he tried to avoid standing on the many mice running about and tried not to stare at the Dreamer.

The many cruel faces of the gargoyles carved on the walls seemed to frown, and in the paintings of various famous leaders of the Citadel, they one by one turned their heads away in dislike at what passed before them.

"Philo, friend, I can call you friend, can't I?" asked the Dreamer.

"Frankly, I'd rather you didn't call me anything," replied Philo. "We seem to have a plague of mice at the moment, and I don't want any stranger dreams, thank you."

The Dreamer laughed, "You are so innocent. You will soon learn. The ways of power are not easy ways. I have a way to haunt you, by night or day."

Philo looked down and held his tongue. He knew that he couldn't help the Dreamer, but he wondered how a person could become all pervadingly awful, and probably also quite difficult to get rid of. The Dreamer continued to follow him, laughing a hollow, frightening laugh.

Chapter Twenty-Four

After a few minutes of walking in silence, Angelica called out, "Stop."

"Why are we stopping?" asked Birrick.

"There is a family of hedgehogs crossing our path." The pair waited patiently, then Angelica called again, "Wait quietly." This time, Birrick eased down the blindfold. He could see in front a pair of black ballet shoes dancing a strange jig, and a peculiar-looking woman in black growing from the shoes as she danced.

"Why are you here?" Angelica asked the woman.

"I am Queen of the Willies, elf friends, this is my part of the forest," hissed the dancing stranger. The woman pirouetted, twisted, and jumped, barring the way with a beautiful yet wicked grace. The willie asked, "What are you looking for?" She took a broken branch and pointed it at the two of them.

"We're looking for Lamguin, the Blade," said Angelica meekly.

"Down there," hissed the woman, pointing with a branch. "A little further down the path, fifteen paces to Camp Chalice. That's where he rests. When you get there you will know, I will give you visiting rights." The willie pirouetted again, and with one fantastic ballet leap was gone.

Angelica continued to guide Birrick and counted to fifteen out loud. "One, two, three, four, five, six, seven, eight, nine, ten, eleven, twelve, thirteen, fourteen, fifteen. Wait stop."

"What is it now?" Birrick removed his blindfold completely.

"Pay me or feed me," came a loud voice and a loud snort. "Pay me or feed me."

"What is your fee?" asked Angelica.

"Two acorns," came the reply. Birrick realized that he was looking at a large pink and black pig, with a ring through its snout and a very large mouthful of gold teeth.

"Pay me or feed me," said the pig again, and Angelica started to look in her pockets.

"Will this do?" she said, offering a packet of toffee.

"What else do you have?" asked the pig as he swallowed the toffee in one go.

"Err, here is an apple," said Birrick, and throwing it at the animal, the pig dashed off after it. There, only a pace or so from where the pig had been standing was a cavern in an outcrop of rock.

Angelica turned to look at Birrick. "Fool," she said angrily. "You've taken it off." Birrick simply shrugged. "Now, down the cavern, and put that blindfold back on, at once. I'm leading you here, when we get to Lamguin, then you do the talking. Do as you're told." Birrick obeyed, retying the blindfold, and holding onto the rope. Then there was another voice.

"Wait, you must please me. I am a government mole."

"Now what?" snapped Angelica sharply.

"Do you have news from the Citadel?" asked the mole.

"Yes," said Angelica. "The authorities are at risk of noodling, or becoming a drongo, so we need to get to Lamguin pretty quickly."

"Alright then," sighed the mole. "Down you go."

It seemed cold in the cavern, and Birrick, though blindfolded, had the sensation of walking along a downhill slope. After a while, perhaps five minutes, Birrick noticed a smell of roasting hog.

"We are entering the chamber of the square table," whispered Angelica. "After this, if the lords let us in, then you can take off your blindfold. Wait until I say."

As the pair halted, Angelica went down in a curtsey. There was a large square table, with three men, lords, each one wearing long robes and a crown.

One lord, the black Lord Merrick, asked, "What is your business?"

"We have come to keep counsel with Lamguin, my lord, the fate of the Citadel is at stake. Surely our leader has recovered from his psychic illness by now. He is needed, there is a terrible struggle going on."

"If we let you talk to him. what will you ask of him?" The lord with frizzy red hair, Lord Amber, spoke directly.

"We must ask him to return with us to the Citadel."

"And if we refuse you?" A blonde lord, Lord Summer, with a head or corn-coloured hair, looked at them sternly.

"I cannot be held responsible for the consequences, nor can Birrick my friend."

A hand suddenly drew back a red velvet curtain; standing there, holding the curtain was a tall man with close-cut red hair and wearing a gold chain with a key at his neck.

"Lamguin, my lord," said Angelica, curtseying deeply.

"Yes, speaking," replied the tall man. "Why is your friend still blindfolded? He will need to see me to know me. Remove the rag elf, and look at us. We will not hurt you here."

Birrick reached his hands and removed the blindfold. Blinking for a second or two as the place was lit by candles, he looked at Lamguin, then realized and made a bow.

"You two are strong, even reckless to come here. Where is friend Philo?" asked Lamguin.

"Probably struggling with a lot of drugged and noodled elves, right now. The water was tainted with some strange solution, it caused a few nightmares and visions. Also, it may have affected the voting."

Birrick looked at Lamguin as he said this.

"Voting, oh dear," said Lamguin.

"The Academics are planning a takeover. They have tried to capture the Angamon Tarn Monster, what else has happened since I left, I am unsure, but I was directed to find you. And some of the nobles want proof of your DNA. You must return to prove this and to strengthen our hand. You are needed in the office. The Dreamer has sided with the Academics. He has come into the dream life of the Citadel. We need you to be certain of success, otherwise, it just may prove too difficult to outweigh the Academics by force of the mind. If we wait too long, we could become unable to stop them. Even children could be used in science, experimentation could go on without ethics, even life itself may be taken, and magic, instead of being regulated, could go underground." Birrick said all this knowing that he sounded desperate. "The way to the Other World may become lost, as

176

might the sense of the soul. You must come back with us to the Citadel."

"Science could be useful. Why are you so worried?" asked Lord Merrick. "What has caused these events?"

"Power grabbing," replied Angelica. "Power without an even mind. Such power has formed a means of attack. We need to get you back there, quickly."

"And how do you plan to get me back to the Citadel?" asked Lamguin.

"We…er…could go by wisp, I know a few of them," Angelica looked at Lamguin hopefully.

"Funny you should say that," said Lamguin. "I have my wisp; a willow wisp. I'm sure she'd be helpful if I asked. First, however, we must eat, I believe we have a hog roast going my lords. Let's dish up and feast."

So, saying that, Lamguin waved the key, pointed it at the square table, and a set of dishes complete with roasted hog and mugs of mead, pots of vegetables, knives, and forks hovered over the square table, then settled.

"Sit down please friends," said Lord Merrick. "Do you plan to go to the Citadel with them Lamguin?"

"Well,"

"And do you need us to come with you?" Merrick looked at Lamguin. Lamguin chewed his food and paused.

"You must drum up support. You must rouse the druids, the wood elves, the green witches, and the elementals, we will join our minds."

"Oh dear, shall we?" asked Lord Amber.

"Oh yes. You've been infallible up to now," Lamguin smiled.

"So," said Lord Summer, "while we gather the powers, you are off, into the lion's lair so to speak?"

"Quite, I'm looking forward to it. We will have to go back and…er…sort things out."

Angelica held up her mug of mead, "Cheers," she said. "Lamguin, I salute you!" She drank her mugful down in one gulp.

"Is that what you intend Lamguin? Are you in good enough health?" asked Merrick.

"Never felt better, and pleased to help our two young friends here. They have faith." Lamguin's brown eyes were surrounded by a few wrinkles, indicating age, thought Birrick, but also character. When they finished their meal, Lamguin got up.

"You must excuse me," said Lamguin. "I must go and call my wisp," Lamguin left, and the three lords turned their attention on the two elves.

"Angelica, are you from the forest?" asked Merrick.

"Yes, I work in the forest, I know the ways of the woods," replied Angelica with a smile.

"And you, Birrick?"

"I'm from the Other World."

"Then what are you doing here? We've had some strange visitors, but surely no one wants to leave the Other World?"

"Why I…er…have to fulfil my purpose to be re-admitted. perhaps I made a few mistakes and got kicked out!"

"Dear me, an errant elf. Do you miss the Other World?"

"Most of all I miss my mother. She couldn't sing well, but she knew the most wonderful stories. I never knew my father at all. Do you sing?" Birrick asked Merrick.

"Yes badly, in the bath."

Lamguin waited patiently at the entrance to Camp Chalice, as he called his willow wisp from the tree nearby. "Come to me from the willow tree, a wish to be in your company." As he called, he felt a vibration in the air. Putting his finger into his left ear, Lamguin received the message and retreated into the camp waiting for the wisp to appear. As he waited, there was a thickening of the atmosphere, a grey mist gathered, forming a large, sad crying face, crying like a weeping willow with a face of mourning.

"What do you wish?" wept the wisp.

"You must take us to the Citadel. There is a state of emergency."

"How many are coming? I do not like to be bothered, I have to weep over so many things, why should I weep over you?" The sad voice rang like a flute in the silence.

"There will be three of us; one quite small elf, a wood elf, and myself. You will be enough."

"So, you say, bring them up here."

"Then wait. I will get the others, won't be long."

Lamguin returned to the remains of the dinner party as Merrick was busy with his toothpick.

"The willow wisp is waiting. Come, Angelica, come Birrick; we must go."

The three lords stood up as Lamguin and the others prepared to go.

"May good luck be with you," said Merrick, "and all that you wish for come true."

"Thank you. We need to speed off," said Birrick. "I think the Starmen have fallen through the night, so they won't be far away. Our time is now."

Following Lamguin, who had a branch over his shoulder, Birrick and Angelica huffed and puffed up the slope to the cavern entrance where the wisp waited for them. Birrick started humming, and Angelica joined him, humming a hopeful tune. Lamguin was waiting with the wisp.

"Hold on to the branch," said Lamguin to the others. They grasped the willow branch with both hands.

"Take us to the Citadel," said Lamguin. Soon they were enveloped by the grey mist of the wisp's ether and flying through the air to the towers and turrets of the Citadel.

Chapter Twenty-Five

Knocking on the door of the office of rule, the door itself opened with a little push. Philo gasped, before him stood Lugh, Bede, Angelica, Birrick, and Lamguin. Lamguin smiled at Philo, and Philo managed a bow. A loud explosive noise, then another, could be heard coming from outside. Going to the window, Philo could see several Angamon Tarn Monsters flying around dropping bombs. He counted six, swooping over the Citadel. Then a large stone flew through a glass window and landed on the table. It was wrapped in a piece of paper, stuck on with sellotape. Philo picked up the stone and peeled off the tape, Philo read the message out loud, "Give over command to science, the Starmen, and us. How can you refuse? We have sent you the Dreamer as our messenger, give in to us NOW. The Starmen have brought the knowledge of the universe and the Dreamer the knowledge of dreams. We have the power of science; the macrocosm. Let this chance pass and you will all suffer, everyone will suffer. The Dreamer is our ally, speak with him."

Philo looked at Lamguin and wanted to cry. The Dreamer stood there, tall, bald, ready.

"Do business with me," said the Dreamer. "Give in to our demands, we will treat you kindly. With the Starmen, we will control the universe and all of the Present Lands. We have cloned the monster; we can rule through science and dreams. Look out of the window, can you see the silver Starmen? They are waiting for the word, to take over the Citadel. They are armed with powers, the powers of the universe."

Lamguin stamped his foot. "Get out. Get out before I throw you out." There was a silence, and the Dreamer started to stare at Lamguin. Somehow the Dreamer shrank, getting smaller, and vaguer until he was gone.

"Now," said Lugh, "we need to assert our defences, our last defences."

"Yes!" agreed Bede, "and there could be a chance somehow, the days of the Citadel are not over, the future is not forgone, we must hold on."

There was a further knock on the door. "Who is it?" asked Bede.

"It's Dunstan, the photographer, I've got a press release to show you."

"Come in then," called Lamguin. "Pleased to meet you."

The photographer entered, a folder in his hand. Holding it out to Lamguin, Dunstan said, "Just taken."

Opening the buff folder, Lamguin, Philo, Birrick and the others looked at a photograph of strange-looking men with white hair, silver skin, and metallic silver clothes, strangely coloured shapes on their faces and their clothes.

"The Starmen," said Dunstan. "Their eyes glowed like hot coals; how can we repel them now?"

At that moment a loud bang caused the party to jump. The door fell off its hinges.

"It's a near hit, they're too close," said Lugh.

"All I can think of is a psychic shield, or perhaps there is some spell?" said Birrick.

"We do not have time for other defences now. We must trigger the ultimate psychic energy drive."

"We don't have an army anymore, do we?" said Angelica. "But we can call on the forces, the druids, all of nature."

"Yes, but," said Philo.

"But," said Birrick, "to trigger this, we need to make a sacrifice. And what is that sacrifice to be?"

"Well," said Bede. "There is a room, deep in the bowels of the Citadel, where there is a kind of demon, used as a form of torture. You know, the sort of thing we used to scare children with."

"And?" said Lamguin.

"And, to strengthen our psychic defences, and they are all the defences we've got, we need to make a sacrifice to the demon, or, the demon saps our power until we sap his. So, we need someone young, innocent, brave, and willing to confront the demon."

"Which leaves one question," said Lugh, "who or what shall we sacrifice?"

All eyes turned on Birrick.

"There is a place deep within the ruins of the original temple on which the Citadel was built, their lives the Demon of Despair, only to be consulted or sacrificed to in times of great need. You, Birrick, are, after all, the most innocent and knowing here." Lamguin looked at Birrick. Birrick looked at the floor.

Suddenly Philo turned and clapped Birrick on the back. "Well, that's sorted then, and we can start preparing our psychic shield. Not an easy task at the best of times. You,

Angelica, call the wood spirits, the druids. You three, Lamguin, Bede, Lugh, summon your fellow minds, as many as you can call on by telepathy, and we will try to assert a psychic shield over the Citadel. We do not have time for other defences now."

"First," said Lamguin. "We need to join hands to cement our strength. Let's stand in a ring with Birrick in the middle. You, photographer, can take a picture for tomorrow's news."

Shuffling around, Lamguin called out, "Mind the mice. In a circle, that's right." As the group gathered around Birrick, he felt the seriousness of the situation. Explosions happening outside, Starmen at the gates, and he, Birrick somehow at the centre. As the walls shook, he felt small, insignificant, but caught in the eye of the hurricane, and only able to cope through a feeling of inner belief and strength.

"Now, let us take hands in a ring, yes, and close your eyes," commanded Lamguin. "I will begin. With this ring of friends, a message of real hope depends on purity, on second sight, and knowing now what's wrong from right. And in this place, we bring in peace, through gathering natural belief, in hope, in joy, in courage, strength, and on our friends this hope depends. Call your mates, the druids wild, the spirits of the woods, inspired. As we now ask, this hope depends on knowing that our duty bends, the laws, the fates, the woods, the winds, accept this from our friendship ring, a will to ward off evil springs." Lamguin reached out, placing his hand on Birrick's head, "We commend you; we send you."

The photographer took a photograph without warning, making Birrick jump.

"Here is something to take with you, wear it, the patterns are runic." Lamguin held out a silver ring, it fitted Birrick's

Saturn finger. "That is the Talisman of Baracka," said Lamguin. "You have put it on your Saturn digit, indicating serious intent. The photographer will show you the way, Birrick, to the demon, but you must go the last part of your journey alone."

Birrick looked at Lamguin, he knew not to argue.

"In the meantime," said Lamguin, "We have to send out our thoughts to build our shield. We need to sit back to back and meld our energies before sending them out. We will be thinking of you Birrick, our success depends on you as well."

The photographer tapped Birrick on the shoulder. "Coming?" he said.

"Yes," said Birrick. "I suppose so, I wouldn't like to be known as a drongo."

"What's a drongo?" asked the photographer.

"A drongo is a person, or an elf, who is largely useless. Though it hurts me to say it, there may be people, even elves who have so lost their purpose that they are just that."

"A drongo?"

"Yes, just that, useless, and I would not like to be known as a drongo myself. Even I, an elf, have a purpose which I must not fail in, so now let's get going please."

Leaving the group in the office behind, Birrick and the photographer scurried away down a warren of corridors, avoiding many mice, cobwebs, and scowling faces of gargoyles that were carved in the walls.

"Down here," said the photographer, pointing to an open stairwell, from which pervaded an evil smell. The steps seemed well-worn stone, the walls of the stairwell green with lichen.

"Are you coming with me?" asked Birrick.

"No, I am going back to work," said the photographer, "but first I will take your picture here, smile." In an instant, the photographer, Dunstan, had captured the worried look on Birrick's face. "You will be known for this, a bright shining light is with you forever." The photographer shook Birrick by the hand. "The talisman he gave you, the Talisman of Baracka, is significant, and you will need good luck where you are going."

"Is that all you have to say?" asked Birrick.

"Yes," retorted the photographer, turning his back and hurrying off.

As he moved on and downwards, Birrick paused at an old wrought iron mirror hanging on the stairway wall. Though there was only a little light, Birrick could see his reflection, and, even in the darkness around himself, he could see the darkness, the fear in his face. Another face, as he gazed, appeared in the mirror, two very dark eyes in the face of a fox were staring back at Birrick. Suddenly the animal opened its mouth, showing a blood-red tongue, and a sharp set of teeth. Stepping back, scared as fear caught at Birrick's throat, and then determined once more, he forced one foot in front of the other, down the ever-narrowing stairway. Birrick cautiously continued his final descent; trying to keep his spirits up he thought of rainbows, toffee apples, then tried to whistle. But, as he whistled, another voice joined him in his tune. "Who are you?" called out Birrick. "Who are you?" There was no answer. As the hairs on the back of his neck stood on end, he continued in silence.

Water dripped from pipework in the stairwell, the pipes connected the water supply with the Citadel wells. A few drops fell occasionally on Birrick's face, water mingling with the cold sweat of fear. The walls of the passageway came so close together so that Birrick had to turn sideways. He could touch the ceiling with a raised hand. A set of grill bars appeared in an opening, with a metal sign reading, 'Danger this way'. Bending down to crouch, Birrick knocked his head on an overhead bar and crawled into a stinking dark enclosure.

Birrick knew that he was in a room a little like a cellar. As his eyes adjusted to the darkness, he heard a rustle and then made out a shape moving towards him. Hesitating, Birrick could make out a pair of eyes, which glowed red like two pinpricks of neon light. Around the eyes there seemed to be a figure, in the shape of a man, perhaps, or was that a fox face on a man's body? The creature smiled and showed a mouthful of silver teeth.

"Come to see me, have you?" asked the demon, quite quiet in the tone used, but also sinister, speaking in a loud whisper.

Scared, Birrick could hear his voice rising, "I'm here to... er...er..."

"Make an offering? You, elf, an offering? A sacrifice for me?" Again, the gleaming smile made Birrick's flesh creep. The only light seemed to come from the creature. Then Birrick noticed his ring, it had a faint glow. The creature came right up to Birrick, and the smell was so bad that Birrick wanted to turn and run. With a cracking sound, the demon suddenly lashed out with a whip, leaving a mark on Birrick's face. Stunned, Birrick felt a strong impulse to hit back, or beg but knew that he could do neither. As the demon dragged Birrick by the neck, holding him up high to get a good look at him, the creature said, "Young tasty meat," laughing softly to itself.

Birrick struggled but realized that he was no match for the evil-smelling demon. Trying to hit out, first with his right fist, then his left, Birrick's arms were not long enough to do damage to the creature. Birrick missed the target. The two red eyes glowed, and the cruel mouth grinned showing its fierce incisors. Putting his hand to his neck to claw at the demon's grasp, Birrick's fingers touched the medal, and he felt a prickle of hope in his fingertips, a sensation of his force.

"How long have you been living like this?" Birrick asked the demon.

"I am here from the Underworld, a place where there is much darkness, just like this." Placing Birrick on a table, all the while looking at him with a mesmeric gaze, the creature asked quietly his question.

"Can you kill people Birrick? Can you do this for another? can you give your soul to me? Can you serve me, a demon? If I suck out your soul, would you promise never to try to leave?" The demon grinned as he spoke.

Birrick closed his eyes, waiting, but it seemed like an eternity of hopelessness. In his mind, Birrick could see a bright blue light, and he heard the words of the photographer, "A bright shining light is with you." Opening one eye, Birrick pointed his Saturnian finger at the demon, whispering, "Lumini vici." A brilliant ray coming from Birrick's finger hit the demon full in the face. Stepping back in surprise, the ring on Birrick's Saturnian finger glowed brightly. Turning around, Birrick could see a wall of flames, and a hand extending from the flames, holding an apple. The hand beckoned; Birrick grabbed the apple, bit into it, then threw the rest at the creature. The apple burst in the creature's face. Galvanised into action, Birrick started to curse, " Incendia furcifer, credo vos mendax in sanguinarium, in sanguine, in prave voles, incendia." A flame ball enveloped the demon, which screamed and twisted as it burned, running into the wall of flames, and vanishing from sight.

Then there was nothing, only quiet, and a figure dressed in gold, the Guardian, was standing at the entrance to the cellar. "Congratulations elf-friend, you have surpassed my expectations and predictions. The demon will be weaker now, so that the evil, the dark side, can be overcome by good. Evil attracts evil, good attracts good, though sometimes light draws darkness to it. Your soul is strong, there is a light in you, which is why you have withstood the assault made. Take my hand and count to three, we will soon be home."

Birrick stood in the cellar counting, one, two, three. A feeling of elation, of happiness, flooded him, and he found himself standing in warm bright sunlight. Before him was a wonderful fountain, and a wolf came to drink from the water, before trotting up to Birrick, then sitting with its head on one side.

"Crimthain," said Birrick, and a rainbow danced in the million droplets of spray from the fountain, while he bent to stroke his old friend.

Chapter Twenty-Six

In the high office the friendship ring sat, back-to-back, hands joined together in silent thought. The whole group, linked by mind power, with druids, wood wisps, elves, witches, and people of the forest, projected a conjoined ring of light around the Citadel. The shining halo, so bright and of beautiful luminescence, repelled the Starmen, the academics, the clones. Once more the Dark Dreamer stood before them, flickering. "Now, I will remain in your mind, and you will not be rid of me so easily. I am in the wind, the night sky, the strangest of your dreams." As he vanished a light like multi-coloured crystal filled the room, the bombing came to an end, and the dark forces returned to their hideaway on the Road to Nowhere where the academics kept their lair. Lamguin smiled a beaming smile, looking at his fellows with pleasure. "It is finished, for now at least. Isn't it time for that DNA test?"

Bede looked at him. "Oh yes, I'll take a lock of your hair, and have it investigated, here," and Bede fished a set of scissors out of a draw and cut off a ginger sample from Lamguin's head.

"It's quiet," said Angelica in a small voice; going to peer out of the broken window. She could see that the streets of the

Citadel were empty, except for the rubble and glass from damaged buildings.

"We will need to repair the damage done," said Lamguin, "but first let's make off to the Coven Bar where we can drink hot chocolate and discuss tactics. We will have more to do before we are rid of this problem of the White Beast and his allies. There will be other commotions, or plots, or confrontations."

"You know," said Philo, as they sat in the bar, playing frog races with several pet frogs kept for the staff, "I will miss Birrick. That elf was some good."

"Yes, so will I," said Angelica. "He was no drongo or noodle. He had guts, and I think he will be back."

"How do you know?" replied Lamguin. "Even I would like to know where he's gone. But for now, a toast, to Birrick, our absent friend, and the Other World." They raised their tankards, crying out, 'to the other world' and drank until they had cream on their noses and chocolate froth on their mouths.

The next day, the pictures which the photographer submitted were printed in the press. At a meeting with Lamguin, the lords, monks, and elves celebrated the return of their leader, along with the lessened threat of the Starmen, and academics, the darker side of science. The stripey witch at the bar announced her last day of community service. Lamguin, taller than any other member of the Citadel was reunited with his friends from Camp Chalice; Merrick, Summer, and Amber. A few witches flew around the Citadel, joyriding on their broomsticks. "Take this," said the stripey witch to Philo, holding out a five-pound note. "Put this behind your mirror, your coffers will never be empty, and you will never be short of toffee again." Philo laughed and thanked her; later he stuck the note behind his shaving mirror. Also, she gave him a copy of the 'Daily Augur'. On the front page was a picture of Birrick as he descended the stairs to visit the Demon of Despair.

"On the second page, they give you all a wonderful write-up, the light will shine on you and the Citadel." The witch smiled at him, and Philo felt able to smile back, his first grin in a long time.

The government soothsayer got out his piano accordion and played an elfin jig; Philo and Angelica took a turn in leading the elves in a merry midwinter dance. The Angamon Tarn froze over, and the elves went skating on the icy tarn surface, a public holiday throughout Yuletide gave the government rest and a day or two off.

Far, far away on the other side of the rainbow, Gabriel, Raphael, and Uriel took a good look at the return of Birrick to this, their spiritual realm. Birrick, accompanied by Crimthain, sat patiently in a hand-made magical circle while the three important angels looked down on him.

"Strange, and even strangers have come here Birrick, yet you have come here, and we did not intend having you here again!" Uriel spoke in an unkindly tone, causing Birrick to scowl.

"Do you have a passport?" Gabriel asked.

"No, I don't," replied Birrick, "and I didn't think I needed one, my mother is here somewhere, isn't she?"

"Well, you have been away sometime Birrick, things have changed here, for us as well as for you." Raphael gave Birrick a serious look, causing Birrick to shiver.

"Where's Michael?" enquired Birrick.

"Oh, he's gone on an expedition to discover a cure for cancer, while the rest of us guard the eternal doorway. Not everyone is allowed through, Birrick sometimes we send scoundrels or undesirables back!" Raphael folded his wings as he spoke.

"But that's not fair, I've been on a quest, struggled with a demon, and found the stone of second sight. I'm tired of trying!"

"And where do you think you came from before you got here, back in the deep, deepest past, where time never stops and where you never listened. What do you think you were doing in the past, Birrick? You came here from somewhere else; inside you, you wished to be here, but in your earliest memories, where were you from?" Uriel's eyes gleamed as his gaze pierced Birrick's mind.

"But wasn't I just an elf? Here, you know, having a nice time?"

"Listen Birrick," said Uriel. "Relax, close your eyes, I will count backwards from ten, nine, eight, seven, six, five, four, three, two, one. Where are you now, Birrick?"

In his mind's eye, Birrick could see a vast lake. A small woman with dark hair rowed in a canoe slowly towards him. The canoe was surrounded by swans. One black swan seemed to be leading the canoe as it swam out in front. As the early morning stars glittered, the lake shimmered with a silver mist. The dipping of the paddle in the water made a faint sound, echoing in the quiet. The woman started to sing, and then she spoke to Birrick from the canoe.

"I am your sister, Aisha." her voice seemed a deep low voice. "I have come to bring you back your childhood, your innocence."

"But I'm not innocent," replied Birrick.

"Don't you want to be? Don't you want to stay here? If you don't want to return to a state of innocence now, then you will have to leave. If you do not give up what you know, then you cannot stay, well?" She spoke with an impatient tone.

"I don't know, but I do know that I'm not an innocent."

"Are you willing to return to a state of blamelessness, meekness, kindness, unearthliness? Say now."

Aisha looked at him sadly. "You are my brother, though you do not know me I am your friend."

"No, I cannot give up being myself."

"Dear me, Birrick, then you will have to go. The Guardian will come for you, and return you to the Present Lands, you will have to do her bidding on the earth plane. You aren't ready to give up the world, the Spiritus Mundi has left its mark on you, in your mind. There is, even more, to be done, the gyre is widening between here and there, you must turn back."

"But I want to stay, I'm from here!"

"Why won't you give up wanting things?" His sister Aisha stood up in the canoe, pointing at him. "Into the gyre you go," she said it like a curse. "you are not ready yet."

Birrick started to spin, rotating in some strange vortex of wind, which carried him with it into the chasm between the Other World and our world. As he spun, he could see birds, bats, dragons, and a black swan, whirling with him. He could see the demon's awful face with its revolting teeth. Masks that seemed to laugh, witches stretching out their fingers to catch at him.

A voice inside his head said, "Take my hand." Groping outwards, pushing against the wind, a soft sensation, a gentle presence took hold of Birrick. He recognized the voice of the

Guardian, though he could not see her, and he knew it was her by the one green eye which he could see in his imagination. Already he knew that heaven and hell were a state of mind.

While sleeping that Yuletide night, yet again Sally saw the white-robed woman, wearing a holly and mistletoe crown. Appearing in a golden mist, and festooned with garlands of wild blossoms, the Guardian looked down on Sally, who lay twitching and muttering in her sleep.

"Is it my turn?" asked Sally.

"No, not yet you're not ready. But thank you for your patience, and for returning Birrick to us, it was a struggle for him, and so will many things be such for you. You have a world within you, with this knowledge you will become stronger, and more certain of yourself."

"Here I am," and Birrick stepped out from behind the Guardian, "and here is the last secret, the doorway is in your mind, you will see me in your dreams, the final secret is in your dreams, believe it." He stretched out a hand, holding an envelope.

When Sally woke in the morning, there was the cat, Teabag, familiar and furry on the bed. She arose, shaking herself with disbelief. Then, as she looked for her wristwatch on the bedside table, she noticed the moonstones, an apple, and an unopened plain envelope. Tearing it open, she took out the scrawled note inside. "Life is a force that lives through the force of life in you, and magic is a science that isn't yet come true. Live your life as you wish, but do no evil, speak no pish. Should any ask you why we're here, the answer's in the atmosphere, and if you think dreams don't come true, then in this message is our clue." Sally sighed, looked at the note again, and put it in her secrets box. Left as she was, with the proof and the moonstones, she smiled to herself. In the garden outside, among the branches which fell in a recent storm, and drenched with melting snow, a stone elf sat, sitting watching the flashing goldfish in the garden pond.